Megan Sparks

Books in the
Roller Girls series

Falling Hard
Hell's Belles
In a Jam
Boot Camp Blues

Megan Sparks

Roller Girls

In a Jam

With special thanks to Alexandra Diaz

First published in 2013 by Curious Fox,
an imprint of Capstone Global Library Limited,
7 Pilgrim Street, London, EC4V 6LB
Registered company number: 6695582

www.curious-fox.com

Series created by Hothouse Fiction
www.hothousefiction.com

Cover designed by Jo Hinton-Malivoire, original concept by
www.spikyshooz.com
Illustrations by Allan Campbell

ISBN 978 1 78202 034 9

1 3 5 7 9 10 8 6 4 2

A CIP catalogue for this book is available from the British Library.

Typeset in Baskerville by Hothouse Fiction Ltd

Printed and bound by CPI Group (UK) Ltd, Croydon, CRO 4YY

Special thanks to Matty, for everything.

Chapter One

"Goooooal!" the announcer shouted. "The Liberty Height Stags now lead the Prospect Park Panthers 3-2 in the final game of the season!"

Annie squealed and hugged her best friend next to her. "Did you see that, Lex? My boyfriend scored a brilliant goal!"

My boyfriend. Just the sound of those words on her tongue made her tingle with excitement. Tyler was by far the fittest guy at Liberty Heights High School. He had irresistible blond hair that always seemed to fall just right and green eyes that Annie could gaze into for hours. And his body … wow! Lean and muscular, he was perfect. And he was all Annie's. She couldn't believe her luck.

Lexie grunted and looked up briefly from her sketchbook.

"He's awesome. Can we go now?"

"Course not," Annie said. The cheerleaders came out and did a little number led by Annie's favourite person in the world. Not. Blonde, popular, and with a personality to match the Wicked Witch of the West, Kelsey had been vicious to Annie since she'd moved to Liberty Heights. They'd got off to a bad start just because Annie had accidentally knocked into Kelsey on her rollerblades. Their relationship had got even worse when Annie turned down a place on the cheerleading squad in order to play roller derby instead, the best sport on four wheels. No, the best sport ever, full stop.

Annie definitely couldn't leave the match now. Not with Kelsey prancing about, thrusting her hips and sticking her chest out as the cheerleaders danced. Kelsey had made it all too clear she wanted Tyler for herself.

"Come on, Lexie," Annie said. "There's only ten minutes left. And this is for the regional championship. Besides, what kind of person leaves before the end of a match?"

Lexie let out a breath that hung white in front of her mouth. "A cold one? It's got to be below zero."

Annie put her arm around her best friend and gave her shoulders a rub. It was pretty cold. In London, where Annie had grown up, it wasn't often this cold. But Annie figured she might as well get used to the weather. She had moved here a few months ago with her dad. Although she missed her mum and England, Liberty Heights, Illinois had some great things going for it and a little bit of cold wasn't going to send her packing.

Annie kept watching Tyler and the match while trying to comfort Lexie. "Pretend you're Vincent van Gogh and can't afford heat in your garret, but you're on the verge of finishing your masterpiece."

"No good, I can't feel the pencil to draw any more." Lexie flexed her hand to get the blood flowing again.

Annie tore herself away from the game for just a second to glance at her friend. Lexie's fingers poking out from fingerless gloves did look a bit blue. Lexie was passionate about her art and never missed an opportunity to work on it. *Maybe*, Annie thought, *she'd enjoy the match if she gave it a chance.*

But Annie wasn't going to say that to her best friend. Lexie and sports were like ice cream and garlic; they just didn't go well together. The last thing Annie wanted was to argue with her.

"Tell you what. Stay with me, just until it finishes, and I'll make you the most gorgeous hot chocolate you've ever had when we get back to Rosie Lee's."

"Fine." Lexie was pawing at the page of her sketchbook, struggling to turn it. "But it better have lots of whipped cream."

"Well, yeah. You know my dad makes it himself." Annie imagined the freshly whipped cream and decided that she might just have to enjoy a gourmet hot chocolate too.

After Annie's mum and dad separated, Dad had decided to return from London to his hometown in Illinois to follow his dream of opening up an English-style café. It was called Rosie Lee's, Cockney rhyming slang for tea. While it had got off to a slow start, business was steady now, especially with the Christmas season approaching.

It had been a hard choice for Annie to choose which parent she wanted to live with. She had grown up in London and definitely felt British, but Dad pretty much raised her single-handedly while Mum worked at her law firm. Dad had always been there for Annie and she couldn't imagine life without him, even if it meant leaving the familiarity of England. Still, Annie couldn't help but hope that maybe her parents would get back together one day.

Annie got to her feet as the Panthers pushed forward, trying to score a goal, but before it got to the keeper, Tyler somehow soared a metre into the air to head the ball back to Javier. Great play!

Five minutes left on the clock and Annie couldn't keep her eyes off the pitch. The ball was going back and forth between the teams, but the Stags still held on to their one goal lead. If they could keep it up, Annie might be kissing a regional soccer champion tonight. Annie let out an excited high-pitched squeal and Lexie responded with a sound of exasperation.

Annie offered Lexie her scarf, but Lexie shook her head. Poor Lexie. If only she could enjoy the game. There had to be a way to make her feel more connected.

"Did I tell you what the team did to the coach?" Annie smiled at the memory of Tyler telling her the story. "Tyler and Ethan bought a live turkey from a farmer the other day and put it in the coach's front garden. The coach freaked out when he came home. The bird started chasing him and wouldn't let him get in the house. The coach had to call animal control and they spent hours chasing after the bird through the neighbourhood!" Annie laughed as she imagined the scene.

"Hilarious," Lexie muttered.

"Don't worry, they caught the turkey and took it to an animal sanctuary."

This time Lexie grunted but didn't look up from her sketch. Maybe it was more than just the cold. Maybe Lexie and her mum were fighting again. Although Annie got along well with Lexie's mum, she knew Mrs Jones wished her unconventional daughter would be more normal. It wasn't fair how parents always wanted their kids to be different to who they were. Annie had the same problem with her mum back in London.

She hugged her legs to her chest and tugged on the hat that covered her long brown hair. OK, maybe it was a bit colder than she admitted. That was the disadvantage of being so tall (five foot eleven and a half) and slim. There was nowhere to store body heat. Everyone had already warned her about the Midwestern winters and it was only November. At least there wouldn't be any more soccer games until next autumn.

Annie glanced at the sketchbook again. Instead of complimenting Lexie's artwork, Annie frowned at the sketch. Lexie's gloved hands were covering most of it.

"Hey, what's that?" Annie asked, reaching over for the sketchbook.

Lexie quickly flipped the book over to hide what she had been doing. "Nothing. Just something I messed up on."

Annie didn't know what to say. She'd seen the sketch for the briefest second when Lexie had moved her hands. Still, it was long enough to know what she saw: a soccer player with an uncharacteristically large head, cheesy grin, and a speech bubble that said, "I'm so awesome." It could have been any of the players, but Lexie was too good an artist not to make him clearly identifiable. Even without the exaggerated cheekbones and the perfect hair, Annie still recognized him easily. Tyler.

Annie realized that Lexie didn't really like her boyfriend. But then again, Lexie didn't like most jocks and the attention they got. She was resentful that athletics got much more funding than the arts. But getting together with Tyler was one of the best things that had happened to Annie since she moved to the United States. Surely Lexie could make an exception and like this one particular jock. Annie knew, though, that it wasn't exactly one-sided. Tyler thought Lexie was a bit eccentric (he used the term "weird freaks" to describe Lexie and her friends from manga club). But Tyler read the comics in the newspaper and that was kind of close to the graphic novels Lexie read. They had that in common at least. Annie really liked both of them and giving up one for the other wasn't an option. Maybe if they spent more time together, they'd realize how great the other was. They would just have to find a way to get along. Besides, they did have another important thing in common...

Annie.

Chapter Two

"I still can't believe we won!" Annie danced around Lexie, half with excitement, half to warm up, as they headed to her dad's café. "I was sure that last shot was going to go right in. If Tyler hadn't cleared it, it would have been a draw."

"We call it a tie," Lexie mumbled.

Annie frowned. Normally Lexie didn't correct her British terms. In fact, Lexie often tried to incorporate British words into her own vocabulary. For instance, Lexie now went to the "loo" instead of the "bathroom".

She's probably just cold and hungry. Some people got all grumpy when they felt like that. Dad was a miserable old git if he worked too hard and forgot to eat. Annie linked her arm through Lexie's and started singing her favourite Queen song, "Don't Stop Me

Now", to cheer her up. By the time they got to Rosie Lee's, Lexie was smiling.

The café was half full when they walked in. Across the black and white chequered floor was a display case stuffed with mouth-watering goodies. Lexie had painted an amazing mural of a double-decker London bus with famous Brits waving from it that gave the café enough hipness to be a hangout for young as well as older customers. Lexie plonked herself down at a table while Annie went into the kitchen. One of the regulars, Simon, was chatting with Dad through the kitchen serving hatch while Dad rolled out the dough for raspberry white chocolate croissants. Not only was Dad the best cook in the world, he loved talking to everyone. Two great qualities for running a café.

Also, it didn't hurt that he never took himself too seriously and was always being goofy.

As soon as he saw Annie, Dad straightened his shoulders and gave an evil laugh. "At last, my victim has arrived. Here, try this."

He reached for a cheddar cheese scone and tried to shove the whole thing in Annie's mouth. Annie extracted the scone as Dad and Simon laughed at her startled expression. She took a normal-sized bite and savoured it. It was delicious. But she wasn't about to say that to Dad; it'd just go straight to his head.

"Hmm, a bit salty, isn't it?"

"You see? That's what I thought too, but Simon," Dad exaggerated his friend's name, "*Simon* thought it was perfect."

"Just face it, Dad, you're not." Annie gave him a condescending pat on his arm.

"Inconceivable!" Dad spluttered in mock indignation.

Now it was Annie and Simon's turn to laugh. Annie gave her dad a kiss and exchanged her school bag for an apron. The oven timer went off and she pulled out some gorgeous-smelling chocolate chip cookies. Dad scolded her when she placed two of the hot cookies on a plate instead of letting them cool first. Annie just smiled sweetly – Dad did the same thing when there weren't customers around. In their minds, there wasn't anything better than a cookie piping hot from the oven. Especially when it was chocolate chip.

Annie devoured hers and set the other in front of Lexie, who was warming up her hands with her breath. "I'll get that hot chocolate going," Annie said.

"Awesome," Lexie said with a grin, looking the happiest she'd been since school ended for the day. Annie smiled back. Amazing what a bit of chocolate could do for anyone's mood. Annie turned to prepare the café's signature drink: steamed milk, Dad's own hot chocolate mix (cocoa, vanilla infused sugar, and pinches of cinnamon, cayenne, and salt), mini marshmallows, and lots of homemade whipped cream.

Annie had just finished adding the whipped cream when the bells attached to the door chimed the arrival of a customer. She glanced over her shoulder and beamed. No, not any customer.

Tyler.

Following behind him came his usual entourage of teammates and cheerleaders, including Kelsey. Annie didn't know why *she* had to come. Kelsey would only complain about how fattening everything was. But then she'd steal bits from the cute boys' plates so the calories wouldn't "count". Or something. Annie had no idea how Kelsey's mind worked. Or if it even did.

She set Lexie's hot chocolate down on the counter before greeting Tyler. "Hiya! How did you get here so quickly? Lexie and I only just made it back."

Tyler dangled the keys to his sports car in front of her and winked. "They're called wheels, babe."

Annie grinned. Tyler knew how strange she found it that everyone drove at sixteen here and loved teasing her about it. Driving age was seventeen in the UK, but in London most people waited until they were older to learn how to drive. Before she could reply to his cheeky comment, he came behind the counter to give her a long snog. There was a definite "eww" that might have come from Kelsey but Annie barely noticed. Tyler's kisses always made her forget everything. When he let go, she had to steady herself against the counter, her legs too weak to hold her up.

"Come sit down." Tyler gestured towards the three tables his gang had pushed together, with their regional championship trophy on the top.

Annie looked around. There weren't any new customers. The empty tables had been cleared and wiped. The display case was full. She grabbed a tray of mugs and the coffee pot, and a plate of assorted cookies, and scooted around the counter. Even though she had just got there, she supposed she could take a mini break.

As soon as she set everything down, Tyler pulled her onto

his lap even though there was a free chair next to him. Annie blushed, not sure what to do. It was a bit awkward. Standing they were almost the same height (actually Annie was an inch taller) but on his lap, she felt like she towered above him. Then there were the other reasons it was awkward.

If Mum were here, she would have scolded Annie for being inappropriate and demanded she get off him at once. But Mum wasn't here, was she? She was several thousand miles away in London. And Dad was busy in the kitchen. Besides, it wasn't like Tyler was touching her where he shouldn't. Just a hand on her leg that felt oh so nice. If they were alone, she'd lean into his chest and enjoy his arms around her. But since they weren't alone, being on his lap was a good alternative. Especially since Kelsey seemed to seethe with jealousy.

"Did you see me score, babe?" Tyler asked as he emptied four sugars into his coffee.

"You were brilliant. During that last shot, you really psyched out that keeper ," Annie gushed.

"I know, I couldn't believe it," Tyler beamed. "He's one of the top goalies in the state."

"Let's not forget who assisted that goal." Javier sipped from a cup of coffee before reaching for a peanut butter cookie. "This coffee is fantastic, Annie."

"Cheers," she said. "And you were great out there too." Javier was definitely the best player after Tyler and the only freshman on the varsity team. Nice too. He always chatted a bit with Annie. She was about to say something else to Javier but

Kelsey interrupted.

"You're a shoo-in for the All State team," Kelsey said, leaning across the table and showing off more cleavage than should be allowed in a family café.

Tyler laughed the compliment away while Annie pressed her lips together. If only she could make Kelsey back off.

They were all still talking about the game when Lexie appeared at their table.

"Annie, I'm going." Lexie stood in front of her, avoiding eye contact.

"No, please don't." Annie got off Tyler's lap. "I was just going to come over."

"What's that you're wearing? Are you going to a costume party?" Tyler laughed. Javier folded his arms and shook his head disapprovingly. Annie wanted to hide.

There was nothing funny about it.

In the few months Annie had known Lexie, she hadn't seen her best friend wear the same outfit twice. Or rather the same look. Today was no exception. Chunky black Mary Janes, black and white striped thigh-high socks, short red tartan skirt, and white shirt. Today Lexie must have spent hours straightening her wild ringlets and tucking the ends under to form a pageboy hairstyle. A red bow sat innocently on top of her head. Lexie looked like she'd stepped out of an anime film.

"It's an artsy look from Japan. I think it's really cool," Annie defended her friend. Lexie always had a way of looking hip. "What did you call it? Harijoku?"

"Harajuku," Lexie muttered, buttoning up her coat.

Kelsey smirked. "Newsflash! Only total geeks get their fashion inspiration from comic books."

"Oh really?" Lexie said, pretending to sound surprised. "I always assumed you were basing yourself on Two-Face from *Batman*, Kelsey." Lexie pulled the white bobble hat she'd knitted herself over her head and took off. The rest of the table hooted at Lexie's comeback.

"Lexie, wait! Tyler was just kidding," Annie said.

Lexie didn't stop, although when she got to the door, she called out over her shoulder. "Thanks for the hot chocolate, Annie. It really warmed me up."

What? Annie turned to the counter where Lexie's drink was melting over the sides. Oh, crumbs. Annie thought Lexie had known it was there. She ran outside to catch up with Lexie and apologize, but her friend was nowhere in sight. The chill bit into Annie as she shuffled back to Rosie Lee's.

She didn't know what to do. She seriously thought Lexie had known the drink was waiting for her on the counter. She put the mug in the sink and wiped the countertop before going back to Tyler's table. "She's gone."

"Her loss, but you look frozen. Here, let me warm you up." Tyler motioned Annie back onto his lap and held her in his arms as he kissed her. Annie instantly felt better. It was so sweet of Tyler to comfort her. It was just what she needed. She pulled out her mobile phone and tapped in a quick text to her best friend:

Sorry, m8. U always look amazing. You should come to school dressed as Loki from *Thor* tomorrow, just 2 wind Kelsey up ☺

Tucking her phone back in her pocket, Annie decided she'd try to go over to Lexie's later to smooth things over. Now that the soccer season was over, Annie wouldn't have to drag Lexie to any more games, which would help.

Three people came into Rosie Lee's and Annie had to peel herself away from Tyler to serve them. She normally liked helping out at the café, but right now she wished the place made just a bit more money so Dad could hire a proper barista and Annie could spend more time doing the things she wanted. Like hanging out with Lexie and snogging Tyler.

People kept coming in for their after-work treats, sometimes sitting down and enjoying a pumpkin spice scone with a cup of tea, sometimes taking pastries home in a white box. Between making drinks, ringing up orders, and clearing up tables, Annie didn't have time to sit with Tyler and the gang again. She had just cleaned up the counter by the espresso machine when the door jingled.

"Hey, wifey, ready to roll?"

Annie's "derby wife" Lauren swaggered over to the counter and helped herself to a sample of the cheddar cheese scones Dad had put out. Lauren always had a smile on her round face and was wearing a beanie hat that looked like a penguin on top of her spiky brown hair. While Lexie was Annie's all-around best friend, Lauren was her most trusted friend on the rink. They were the only two freshmen on the Liberty Belles roller derby team. Annie had tried some bold moves while playing that she would have never dared if Lauren hadn't been there to help her out. Lauren was definitely the perfect "wife".

Annie glanced at the clock, surprised it was time for roller derby practice already. "Let me just tell my dad I'm leaving."

She hung her apron on a hook, grabbed her coat and bag, and blew a kiss at her dad. She wished she could say goodbye to Tyler in private, but he gave her a long public kiss anyway.

"C'mon, Keith is waiting for us," Lauren urged.

Annie pulled away reluctantly, her face a deep crimson. "I'll call you later," she told her boyfriend.

"You better." Tyler winked and settled back down with his teammates. Annie hesitated for a second. Maybe she could stay with Tyler a bit longer. But then Lauren cleared her throat and jerked her head to the door. Annie sighed and followed her friend.

Keith was Lauren's burly linebacker brother and just as big a sweetie as Lauren. Still, getting on the bad side of your driver, particularly on such a cold November day, was never a good idea.

"Aww, you two are so cute," Kelsey smirked at Annie and Lauren leaving together. "Looks like you have some competition, Tyler."

"Shut up, Kelsey," Annie and Javier said at the same time.

"I don't know why you're wasting your time with that freak." Kelsey pretended she was only talking to Tyler, but her snide voice echoed throughout Rosie Lee's as Annie headed to the door.

"Annie is awesome," Tyler said in her defence.

Annie beamed but Kelsey didn't back down. "But everyone knows roller derby is just for lesbians and losers."

Lauren turned around sharply, her face no longer sweet and smiley. "Excuse me?"

Annie lowered her red face and grabbed Lauren's arm. "Let's go. I don't fancy Coach Ritter's wrath if we're late." Although she secretly wished Lauren would punch Kelsey. Not that Lauren was the type to hit someone.

Not off the roller derby track at least.

Chapter Three

Roller derby was nothing like Kelsey made it sound.

Yes, all kinds of girls were encouraged to play regardless of size, shape, or background, but that's what made it so great: everyone was treated the same. It was the total opposite of the cheerleading squad, where it was an unwritten requirement that you had to be conventionally pretty and skinny.

Coach Ritter had made it very clear when Annie first learned about roller derby that anyone was welcome to join as long as they had the basic skills to play safely. Cheerleading try-outs, on the other hand, had been all about picking the "best" girls. Annie was proud to say that even though she had succeeded in making the cheerleading squad, she had turned it down to play roller derby and hadn't looked back since.

And for good reason. Nothing beat roller derby. Out on the track, four girls from each team would huddle together to form a wall and prevent the other team's jammer from getting past, while trying to help their own jammer get past the other team. After breaking through the pack once, every time a jammer passed opposing players, she'd score a point. It was easier said than done. The blockers did everything they could to stop the opposing team's jammer from passing them. And it was all done on roller skates. The result was a fast-paced, full-contact sport that was seriously fun to play.

Usually Annie looked forward to practices, but not today. Her mind went back to Rosie Lee's, wondering what was going on there. Had Tyler told Kelsey off for her rude remark? While Lauren and Keith chatted about American football, Annie checked her phone four times to see if Tyler had texted. He hadn't. Maybe Annie should contact him. Just a quick text to let him know that his girlfriend was thinking about him. That's wasn't stalker-ish, right?

Yes.

No.

Argh! Annie threw her phone into her bag, unable to make up her mind. It'd be so much easier if Tyler would just text her to start a conversation off. She'd never had a boyfriend before and there were so many "rules" she didn't know.

When they got to the rink, Annie headed over to the skate rental booth where her friend Jesse worked. A skater boy, he liked the emo look and today was no exception with his black hoodie, black skinny jeans, and black chequered Converse. His shaggy black hair hung over his incredibly blue eyes. As Annie waited for Jesse to fetch the sturdy quad skates she regularly borrowed, her mind wandered back to Rosie Lee's.

"I just downloaded this great new album from Cradle the Grave called *Been There*. Heard it?" Jesse asked, passing her the skates.

Annie blinked. She'd been so lost in her thoughts, she'd almost forgotten Jesse was there. "Ah, no. Who are they again?"

Jesse brushed the spotless counter with his hand, no longer looking at her. "Local punk group I was telling you about the other day."

Annie remembered now. Jesse had impeccable taste in music, both in the classics and in new stuff, and was always turning Annie on to new and unknown bands.

"That's right. You were gutted that they were playing at a twenty-one-and-over pub. Any good?" she asked.

"Awesome. You and your dad would dig it. Some great guitar solos he can play on the broom," Jesse teased. Half the town knew about Dad's weakness for blasting rock music and playing the broom guitar while "sweeping" the café after hours. Some Liberty Heights residents still remembered when he was in a garage band as a head-banging teen.

"Great," Annie laughed, although what she really wanted to do was check her phone again. Instead she focused on putting on her pads.

"Hurry up, Annie," Lauren called from the rink where she

25

was already warming up.

"All right," she said, trying to focus on something other than Tyler.

"I can burn you a copy of the album if you like," Jesse offered.

"Cheers." Annie removed her sock from her left foot and pulled on her ankle brace before putting her sock back on. Last month she had sprained her ankle and although it was fine now, the doctor wanted her to wear the brace for extra support. Indefinitely. She tried to remind herself that she should feel proud of her battle wounds, like when she had a brilliant purple bruise on her hip from being knocked over by another skater. But for some reason the bandage always made her feel weak.

She laced up her skates and gave Jesse a little wave before joining the rest of her team out on the rink to warm up. Normally they practised with the whole league but with the championships coming up, the teams often met by themselves now. Not that Annie minded. While most of the roller girls were friendly and supportive, it had been because of a girl named Dee Stroyer – a player on another team – that she now had to use an ankle brace.

Annie changed direction with the rest of her team to skate clockwise. A couple of times, Coach Ritter had got them to play a whole scrimmage going clockwise instead of the usual counterclockwise direction. Annie hoped she wouldn't do that today. It required more muscle work – and brain work – than she felt she had the energy for.

Is Tyler still at Rosie Lee's or has he gone home now? Maybe she should have sent him a text, just to tell him she got to the rink

OK. Although why wouldn't she? Lauren's brother Keith was a great driver.

"Annie, did I tell you?" Sharmila interrupted Annie's thoughts. Always in flawless make-up and the latest fashion, Sharmila was the perfect example of why you shouldn't judge a book by its cover – she might look like she belonged on the front of *Vogue*, but she was one tough roller girl. "My cousins are coming over from London for my sister Priya's wedding."

All thoughts of Tyler and what he was doing now left Annie's mind at the sound of her hometown. "Ooh, whereabouts do they live?"

Sharmila shook her silky black hair and laughed. "Uh, I don't know. I've never been there. My *ammi* is going crazy though getting everything ready since we have relatives coming from all over. You should see what I'm wearing for the wedding: a gorgeous pink silk sari with hand-sewn gold embroidery. I feel like a princess. I swear, there's nothing sexier than a sari."

They skated past Jesse in the skate booth and as he looked up, Annie noticed his blue eyes widen at the mention of a sexy sari.

Not that she could blame him. Sharmila, with her heart-shaped face and striking green eyes, was one of the most gorgeous girls in school. In a sari, she would undoubtedly stop traffic all the way to Chicago.

"I'll be doing Priya's make-up, of course," Sharmila went on as they stopped skating and stretched out their legs. "But she and my mom are fighting about whether she should pierce her nose. It's traditional for women to wear a nose ring when they marry but Priya doesn't like it. It's funny – in most cultures it's the mothers who don't want their daughters to get piercings! I don't know if I—"

"Ladies, this is roller derby, not the social hour." Coach Ritter skated through the row of girls stretching, not looking the least bit impressed. "You can catch up with your gossip on your own time. Has anyone heard from Liz?"

Just as she said that, Liz, the team's captain, came dashing in. Long blonde hair in a mess, one wrist guard on, the straps of a knee pad threatening to come off, one ear missing two of its three earrings, Liz had obviously been trying to get dressed while driving.

"Sorry, sorry I'm late! Had to send a form off for my college applications. When they say there's a five o'clock deadline, they mean Pacific Time, right?" Liz dumped her bag and finished getting ready in less than a minute.

Coach Ritter sighed and shook her auburn head. "OK, I know there's a lot going on with school, and weddings and Thanksgiving coming up, but we still have the championships in a few weeks and this year, we actually have a chance of winning it. If anyone is going to be late for practice, I need to know."

Carmen raised her hand. "I have to work on Thursday so I might be late."

Coach Ritter nodded. Carmen worked more hours than was probably legal at her family's dry-cleaning business. Annie didn't know how her curvy, brunette teammate managed to squeeze in roller derby and still get perfect marks at school. Helping Dad at

Rosie Lee's for a couple of hours after school was hard enough and Annie's marks weren't anywhere close to perfect.

"All right, let's focus." Coach Ritter clapped her hands. "Simon Says sprint to the opposite wall."

Thirteen girls took off at various speeds to the wall. Annie and Holly, a short, feisty girl with flaming dyed red hair, got there at the same time.

"I won, Princess Slowpoke," Holly said with a proud smirk.

"You wish. You were the one lagging," Annie retorted. The two glared at each other before laughing. Yes, they were competitive with each other, but it was all in fun. Like Holly calling Annie "Princess" for her slight resemblance to Kate Middleton.

"Simon Says run on your toe stops."

Here Holly did excel − she practically danced on her brakes. And just to make sure Annie knew she was beaten, Holly blew her a patronizing kiss. Annie rolled her eyes and stuck out her tongue. She'd get her own back.

"Simon Says sidestep. Stop and turn around."

Two girls stopped before they realized Coach hadn't said Simon Says. They laughed good-naturedly and went back to sidestepping.

"Simon Says touch the ground with your hands while lifting your skates off the rink."

There was a roar of laughter as the girls did their own variations. Lauren sat on her bum with her hands behind her and skates lifted up in front. Holly did something that looked like a donkey kicking up its heels while Liz straddled her legs and pressed against the rink to muscle herself a few centimetres off the ground. Annie took the opportunity to practise one of her guilty pleasures: gymnastics on skates. She kicked up into a handstand and walked around Lauren with her legs perfectly straight in the air. When she was ready to come down, she sent a leg over her head in a walkover. The wheels rolled her away gracefully as she stood up. After having to retire from gymnastics last year because she got too tall, it was fun to incorporate moves in the rink whenever she could.

There, Holly, let's see you beat that. Sure enough Holly was shaking her head and trying to hide a surprised grin that Annie had one-upped her.

"All right peeps, now that I've got your attention back, let's get working on forming walls. All of you, huddle together for a game of Blood and Thunder. Using legal moves only, try to knock down or push your teammates out of bounds. If that happens, you're out of the game. Also if you're more than ten feet from the pack, you're also out. Last girl standing is the winner. Ready?" Coach blew her whistle and all at once there was pushing, shoving, and blocking from all directions.

Holly pushed against Annie, but Lauren caught Holly off guard and sent the shorter girl sliding to her knees. Annie skated away to avoid being Lauren's next target. Just because they were derby wives didn't mean Lauren would go easy on her. And there was no way Annie could bring Lauren down. She was too good.

As Annie hovered at the rear of the pack, her mind went back to Rosie Lee's and to what Kelsey had said.

Why was Tyler dating her? She wasn't really awesome, despite what he'd said. OK, so she wasn't ugly, and she was athletic, like Tyler, but was that enough for the most sought-after guy in school to want her?

It doesn't matter why. It's enough that he does like me. He said I'm great. Annie pushed her insecurities aside and dashed to catch up with the pack. Lost in her thoughts, she'd fallen behind and would be dropped from the game if she didn't catch up. There were only three other skaters left: Lauren, Sharmila, and Liz. Lauren saw Annie coming and got ready to block her. Annie dodged, knocking into Sharmila instead, who lost her balance. In a second, all four of them came crashing down to the rink. With no one left standing, there would be no queen of the rink this time.

Coach Ritter blew her whistle while shaking her head. "That was pitiful. It's like you're not even trying. Everyone's mind is somewhere else. Just because we're currently at the top of the league it doesn't mean we're going to win the championship, or even get to play in that bout. Our spot isn't secured yet. Don't get overconfident; we still have a long way to go. Next practice, I don't want to see any slacking off. Laps around the rink for five minutes – go!"

Annie pushed off with her toe stops. As much as she wanted to complain about Coach Ritter's nagging, she knew the coach had a point. In her prime, Coach Ritter had been "Miss Demeanour" – one of the best roller girls in the state. Annie remembered what her gymnastics coach used to say: *"If you want the gold, you can't take your eyes off it or someone else will snatch it up."*

Annie upped her speed and passed three teammates who had been in front of her. She wanted to win and she was going to do her best to make sure it happened. Maybe she didn't have to think about Tyler *all* the time. No matter how good-looking he was. He'd still be there after practice.

She had the boy; now she needed to get a championship of her own!

Chapter Four

Annie jumped in the shower as soon as Lauren and her brother dropped her home. It didn't matter how cold it got, roller derby had a way of working up a sweat unlike any other sport.

Clean and refreshed, she pulled on some flannel bottoms and a comfy sweatshirt for pyjamas. She ran a comb through her wet brown hair and then plaited it into two pigtails. If her plan worked, she'd have wavy hair in the morning. Annie didn't change her look daily like Lexie did, but now that she had a boyfriend, she liked to make an extra effort.

In the kitchen, Dad was slumped on a chair, his eyes closed and mouth half open. The lasagne he'd made last week was defrosting in the microwave. He opened one eye when Annie walked in.

"Your friends sure know how to keep business booming," Dad said as he opened the other eye and stretched. "Thought I was going to have to beat them off with a stick before they went home."

"You did make them pay, right?" Annie demanded. It was one thing for Lexie to get free cookies, but Annie knew her dad couldn't afford to support a dozen teens' food fix, especially hungry soccer players.

"Oh yeah, they covered their tab and Tyler even threw some change into the tip jar."

Annie smiled at the sound of her boyfriend's name. "Yeah, he's good like that."

Not that he needed to at Rosie Lee's. As far as Annie was concerned, Tyler and Lexie both fell into the "no-pay" policy, but he always insisted on covering his share. And Annie's if they went out together. Annie knew that money wasn't an issue for him as his parents were well off, but it was still generous.

"I'm not complaining – it's great for business having them there. It's just that your friends eat a lot, meaning I had more prep to do for tomorrow," Dad went on. "It's hard to keep up with a popular daughter."

Annie smiled as she grabbed the oven mitts to take the lasagne out of the microwave. Dad was right. She was popular. Of course it was all because of Tyler. Because she was dating him, everyone knew who Annie was and wanted to hang out with them both. It was nice and nothing she had experienced before. Back in London, aside from a few close friends, not many girls at school knew who she was. That was because Annie had spent most of her time doing gymnastics instead of socializing.

"I'll help you out all afternoon tomorrow," Annie said. "We'll stock up on everything for the next time they come in."

Instead of saying anything, Dad just gave her a thumbs up; his mouth was full of spinach, beef, and cheese. When he swallowed, he had a much more pressing matter to discuss. He asked in a professorial voice, "And how, might I enquire, are your studies? Are you keeping up with your daily assignments?"

"Like totally." Annie flipped a plait over her shoulder and adopted what she knew was a bad American teenage accent. Playing with voices had always been their special game. "I'll totally, like, get everything done after dinner. In fact on Thursday, I'm gonna, like, go study at Tyler's house."

Dad narrowed his brown eyes. Any sign of tiredness or playfulness were gone from them. "Study? With a boy? I'm not so old that I don't remember what 'studying' really means."

Annie pushed a bit of lasagne around her plate. There was nothing wrong with taking a few kissing breaks. Not that Dad needed to know that. "No really, we will. We're reading *The Taming of the Shrew* for English and he asked me to help him out."

"Aren't you two getting a bit too serious?"

Annie shrugged. "I really like him."

"Right." Dad rubbed his five o'clock shadow. Except that he'd been up since three in the morning and it was now past eight at night so his cheeks were scruffier than normal. "Um, how can I put this? Let's say you're this totally amazing singer.

35

I mean real outstanding vocals, like all heads turn when you open your mouth."

"OK…" Annie squinted, not sure where Dad was going with this. She could hold a tune fine but no one would say she was the next Adele.

"And then there's this other musician, a guitarist let's say, and you and the guitarist decide to form a band," Dad said.

Now Annie was really confused but she went along with it. "OK, so we can make music together."

"No!" Dad shouted, which made Annie jump. Dad took a couple of deep breaths before continuing. "You just, well, you sound OK together and that's fine. You want to keep it that way. Just chilled and low key. But then you're offered a, uh, record deal to make music together. The, um, guitarist thinks it's a great idea, but the singer doesn't want to."

"Is the singer still me?" Annie asked.

Dad's face had turned a dark crimson. "Maybe, yes. Yes, the singer is you. You don't want to sign because that will change everything. But the guitarist keeps insisting and you finally agree. But making music together doesn't feel right and you've, er, lost your groove. Forever."

Annie ran his words through her head again. It didn't make any sense. She loved good music but she had never thought of joining a band. "Dad, I have no idea what you're saying."

"I don't want you to get pregnant or end up with some disease!" Dad blurted out.

The echo of his words rang through the house while Annie

felt the weight of the walls pressing against her. *Please, let me die now!*

"Dad!" Annie blushed. Really! What brought *that* into his head? Oh right, studying at Tyler's. "We're not *that* serious."

Dad's face started returning to a more normal shade of red. He took a huge forkful of lasagne and seemed to swallow it whole. "Good, phew. But just in case, you do know how…"

Annie covered her face with her hands, still waiting for the world to end. This was not the conversation she wanted to have with her dad. Not that it'd be any easier with Mum either. "Yes, I know about it all. They taught us in Year Seven and Mum explained it again when we went shopping for, er … clothes."

Dad ran a hand through his brown hair, making it stick straight up. "Yes, she said she did, but … anyway. Do you, uh, have any questions?"

You mean about losing my groove?

If Annie wasn't so embarrassed herself, she would have relished the sight of her normally confident Dad being so clearly uncomfortable.

"Dad, we're only snogging. Nothing else, I promise."

He seemed to accept that. "Good. But if you ever need to talk to me, or your mother, we—"

Mum. Talk. Crumbs. Annie had forgotten about her Skype date with her mum. The oven said 8.27 p.m. That was 2.27 a.m. in London. Mum should be asleep, but with the late hours she worked there was a chance she wasn't.

"Sorry, Dad. I promised Mum we'd talk today." Annie put

37

her plate in the dishwasher and ran to her room, more than a little relieved she had a good excuse to leave the conversation with Dad behind. She turned on the computer and saw the green bubble in the corner that indicated Mum was still online.

Annie pressed the call button as she pulled the headphones on. A few seconds later, a green monster appeared on the screen.

"Ahh!" Annie jumped, and a pair of familiar blue eyes blinked open. "Mum?"

"Sorry, sweetheart, I must have nodded off. You all right?"

"Mum, you're green!"

Mum touched her face and grinned under the crusty face mask. "Yes, it's avocado. One of my friends said it would rejuvenate me."

Other than on Halloween or in the musical *Wicked*, Annie had never seen a green person. Annie thought about pointing this out, but Mum wasn't like Dad. She might get a bit put out if Annie teased her about her "looks". "I better let you go so you can get back to sleep."

"Rubbish, I'd rather talk to you. Besides, I still have some work to do." Mum was squinting and leaning into the screen a little closer than normal without her glasses on.

"You shouldn't work so much." What Annie left unsaid was that if Mum didn't work so much, she wouldn't have to resort to applying green gunk to rejuvenate herself.

"What else am I going to do? Without you here, work is the only thing I have to pass the time."

"Mum, I..." Annie didn't know what to say. How could she

explain to one parent why she chose to live with the other?

Mum smiled sadly. "I know, you wanted to try out a new life. I understand. One of my biggest regrets is not having taken a gap year to travel the world. But then maybe I wouldn't have met your father and had you."

That didn't help the awkwardness of the conversation and the unspoken fact that Annie had picked Dad over Mum. She tried a different approach. "Maybe you can go to an evening class. Yoga or something. I heard that can be rejuvenating." And then Annie wouldn't feel so bad about her mum working all the time to make up for being home alone.

Mum laughed. "We'll see. But enough about me. How are you? How are your friends? Lexie and the roller derby lot?"

With a pang of guilt, Annie realized she hadn't gone over to Lexie's to make it up to her as she had planned. And she hadn't had a text back from her either, which wasn't a good sign. "Lexie's in a bit of a strop. We, uh, had a misunderstanding."

"Did you try to explain?" Mum suggested.

"I tried. But she left Rosie Lee's kind of quickly." Annie looked down at her fingernails.

"What was the misunderstanding about? Maybe I can help."

"No, it's that…" Annie looked around her room, avoiding her mum's eyes. She really should have just rung, instead of doing a video chat. She hadn't mentioned anything about Tyler to Mum yet, not even that she had a crush on him. Now that she was in a relationship (*Wow, that sounded so grown-up!*), she really couldn't hide him any more. "The thing is, I got a bit distracted. I'm kind of seeing someone. A boy – Tyler."

Mum fumbled with something in the background and all of a sudden reappeared with her glasses over the green mask.

She peered at Annie and said, "Pardon? You have a boyfriend?"

"Yes," Annie mumbled. Mum didn't have to make it sound like it was such a surprising, or horrid, thing.

Mum pressed her lips together in a straight line. "Hmm. You remember that talk we had at Harrods? When you got fitted for your first bras?"

Argh, does everyone have to bring that up today? "Yes, I know about all that. Dad asked the same thing. I'm not a baby, you know."

"I never said you were, I just want you to be safe." Mum forced a smile. "So, tell me about him then."

"Well." Annie twirled the end of a plait around a finger. "He's really fit. And really friendly. He talked to me on my first day of school. He's a great soccer – I mean, football – player, and he's really popular."

"Hmm," Mum said again. "I guess I'll see for myself when I meet him."

"What?" Annie stared at the computer screen in surprise, wondering if she'd heard right.

"I've decided to come visit you in a few weeks. I know you'll be off school for three days because of Thanksgiving and it'll be a good time for me to take time off work before the Christmas madness."

Annie blinked a few more times, taking in the news. "You're coming to visit me?"

"Unless you don't want me to."

"No, of course I do." Annie glanced around her room again. She'd have to do a major clean up before Mum arrived. "It's been ages since I've seen you. Are you staying with us?"

"Your father agreed I could stay in his old room since I hear he's taken over your grandparent's bedroom. He promised me his AC/DC posters have been taken down." Mum gave Annie a big smile, cracking her avocado mask. "It will be great to see each other, won't it?"

Annie hoped so. She missed her mum more than anything. It would be great to show her around and introduce her to Lexie and Tyler, but it might be a bit weird. One of the biggest reasons her parents split up was because Mum worked so much. Even when she was meant to be on holiday, Mum was always checking her work emails. Mum liked to be in control.

But how would that work when she was a guest in her ex-husband's house?

Chapter Five

"I don't get why we have to read this." Tyler slammed *The Taming of the Shrew* on the glass dining room table at his posh house. "All this rhyming poetry crap. Why can't they talk like normal people? It doesn't make any sense." He slouched down into the chair in exasperation.

Annie pushed the copy back towards his hands. His voice had echoed through the house, which was massive even by American standards. She had been given a tour the first time she had been there. It had lasted about ten minutes. She was fairly confident she could find the nearest bathroom, but there were loads of other rooms, like the library and the conservatory, that she would need a map to find again. Such a huge place and they were all alone. She tried not to think about that. She came here, after all, so that they could work on their homework together. Mostly.

Even with their two-year age difference, they were in the same English class. Annie reasoned it was because the British school system started earlier, not because she was particularly clever. "The book's not that bad."

Tyler gave a melodramatic sigh. "That's because you're English. You understand what they're saying."

Annie laughed. "Surely you know that no one speaks like that any more."

"*Surely*, I don't." Tyler teased her in a passable English accent. She pushed him playfully but he grabbed her hand and turned her towards him. "I love the way you talk. It's really sexy."

Annie's heart gave an internal squeal as he started kissing her. But no, they couldn't get distracted. They had to get their homework done. If Tyler didn't get a passing grade on his essay, his place on the soccer team could be in jeopardy because players needed to maintain a minimum Grade Point Average. Hating herself for doing it, Annie straightened back into her chair although she could feel his presence next to her, his body heat tingling on her arm.

"We really need to crack on if you want to get a good mark," she said.

Tyler kissed the hand he was still holding and sighed. "You're right. OK, so tell me about this shrew thingy. Is it one of those plays where everyone dies?"

Annie knew she should make him read the play, but it didn't hurt to give him an overview. In fact, that might be exactly what he needed to understand it. "No, it's a comedy, not a tragedy. So there's this girl Katherine, the shrew—"

Tyler rested his head in his hands. "What's a shrew again? Like a mouse, right?"

Annie blinked. Maybe this would be harder than she thought. "Yes, shrews are rodents, but in this case it means a grumpy and bitter woman. Katherine doesn't get on with anyone and her sister, Bianca, who's lovely, can't get married until Katherine does. Then along comes Petruchio who wants Katherine for her dowry and likes the idea of 'taming' Kate so he marries her to prove a point."

"Fascinating," Tyler drawled sarcastically but the mischievous look in his eyes was so sexy that Annie chose to ignore his tone. "And you've already read the whole thing? You're so smart."

Annie blushed under his stare. "I haven't read it all yet, but Mum and I saw an all-male production of the play in a park in London. It was brilliant because it was how it must have been in Shakespeare's time when they didn't allow women on stage." Annie remembered the men in their wigs and them walking in dainty steps. "The bloke who played Katherine was amazing. His speech at the end made it seem like Katherine wasn't tamed, but was taking the micky." Annie booted up her laptop. "I'm going to write about how the ending is ironic."

Tyler looked like he had barely heard what Annie had said, and just stared at her teasingly. Annie took a deep breath just to keep focus. Not that it helped. His bare foot was playing footsie with hers.

Annie closed her eyes for a few seconds. She could focus on her homework. She really could. "What are you going to write about?"

Tyler didn't even pick up the book to thumb through it for inspiration. She could feel his eyes on her. "You. 'Shall I compare thee to a summer's day?'"

"That *is* Shakespeare, but it's not a quote from this play," Annie corrected with a smile. She wouldn't, couldn't, look at him.

"So?" His foot snuck up her jeans, just above her ankle. Who knew that part of her body was so sensitive? She had to bite her lip to keep from sighing with pleasure.

Instead, she started typing frantically, not even aware of what she was writing. "No really. You need a topic."

Tyler finally stopped trying to distract her and turned to his computer. "Maybe I can talk about how this shrew is kind of like a mouse?"

Annie wasn't sure how well that would go down with Ms Schwartz, their English teacher. But on the other hand, she was so Bohemian, that might be exactly what she was looking for. "Could work, if presented the right way. Let's work for half an hour and then we'll take a break. Deal?"

"Yeah, whatever." Tyler slumped in front of his computer and began clicking at the keys, although his foot kept up with its game of footsie. As did hers. After all, she could multitask.

Sort of.

Ten minutes into the writing, she glanced over to see how he was doing. Not well. In the background there was an open

45

document with the title: "Shrews: How Women are Like Mice". Annie couldn't tell how much he'd written because in the foreground of the screen he had a silent game of pinball with a high score.

Maybe they needed a break.

Annie finished her paragraph quickly and saved her essay. There was loads of time to finish it.

"I've got a new idea. This won't get you out of reading the play, but maybe it'll help you understand it." Annie pulled out a copy of the movie *10 Things I Hate About You*. She had brought as something they could reward themselves with when they'd finished their homework, but maybe it wouldn't hurt to put it on now. "It's very loosely based on the play, but some of the themes are the same."

"Cool." Tyler closed his computer with a huge sigh of relief.

They moved into the "recreation room", which had a massive TV built into the wall and surround sound speakers. It was like being at the cinema but with much comfier seats. Tyler used the five remotes to get everything going before gesturing for Annie to sit next to him. She leaned into his chest as he kept an arm around her. There was no denying this was much nicer than sitting in front of a computer.

They skipped the adverts and thirty seconds into the film, Tyler was kissing Annie's neck. Then her collarbone. Ooh, that was nice. His hand had shifted her shirt just a bit so he was running his fingers on her bare waist and still kissing her neck. Oh, what the heck, she'd seen the film before.

She shifted to kiss him full on the lips. A long, sweet kiss she felt all the way to her bare toes. In the background the movie continued playing, but she had no idea what was going on. His hands switched from her back, to her hair, to cupping her face as she leaned into his gorgeous chest and ran her own hands down his strong arms.

From the dining room, Annie's phone rattled against the glass table with an incoming call. Annie stopped kissing Tyler but didn't break away from him. She didn't want to be one of those people who stopped everything for an incoming call; she didn't want to be like her mum. But what if it was an emergency?

Tyler kept his arms around her as she wondered what to do. She was just about to ignore the call when she caught sight of the time on the television set. The phone stopped ringing but she knew who it had probably been. Lauren. Asking if Annie needed a ride to practice.

She slumped back down against Tyler and sighed. "I've got to go. I have roller derby in fifteen minutes."

Tyler brushed a strand of hair from her face and gave her a sad look that reminded her of Lauren's basset hound, Prudence. "Don't go."

Annie averted her eyes. He looked so disappointed it wrenched her heart. "I have to. With the championships coming up…"

His hand stayed on her face, drawing little swirls on her cheek with his fingertips. "I know, but it's just that we don't get to spend much time together."

True. Between school, sports, and helping out at Rosie Lee's, it wasn't very often that it was just the two of them.

"They're counting on me," Annie said, although she didn't make any effort to move. She and Tyler were having so much fun. And there was still half of the film to "watch".

"But it's just a practice, and you're already really good. It won't matter if you don't turn up just this once. Please?"

Annie took a deep breath. She hated missing practice. Even when she sprained her ankle last month, she had still helped out the team as a non-skating official.

On the other hand, he had a point. Yes she was a good jammer, but Holly was just as good or even better (not that Annie would admit that to her). And there were others who played jammer too. They could practise without her and be fine.

"I suppose I don't have to go." She snuggled back against him as he held her tight.

"It's just that you're so great. I don't want to be away from you." He gave her his heart-stopping smile. "I'm glad you're here."

"Me too," she grinned and leaned into another lingering kiss. What was one little roller derby practice in the grand scheme of things? The team could get by without her. Just this once.

Chapter Six

Annie read through her English essay as she slumped against the lockers at school on Friday morning. She'd got home late from Tyler's and had stayed up even later to get the homework done. It certainly wasn't her best. If she had a few more hours she could make it better, but she didn't. It would have to do. She felt like her mum, working until all hours of the night, except Philippa Bradley always did a good job when she pulled an all-nighter.

Annie put the essay back in her bag. Grabbing the books she needed for her morning classes, Annie slammed the locker shut and jumped at the sight of the person next to her.

Feet shoulder width apart, arms crossed over her chest, Lauren gave her a disappointed scowl. "Where were you yesterday?

I tried calling you. You missed practice."

Annie couldn't look at her teammate. "Yeah, sorry about that. I, uh, had quite a bit of homework."

"Really? I thought you said your classes here were easier than in England."

Annie shifted her weight from one foot to the other. "Well, I was kind of helping Tyler. You see, he didn't understand—"

Lauren shook her head. "I get it. I just never thought you'd be the kind to bail on your team. Especially for a guy. He wouldn't have done the same for you."

Annie was too tired to defend Tyler. Not that she had a case. She hadn't thought about it last night but now that she did, she knew Lauren was right. Tyler lived for his soccer team; she couldn't see him missing out on practice because of her. *But it's different for him*, she argued with herself. *He knows that soccer is his best chance at getting into a good college.*

Annie put a hand on Lauren's arm. What Tyler would have done was beside the point. Annie had made her choice; she had wanted to hang out with him. "I'm really sorry – time slipped by and…"

"You should have called," Lauren insisted. Annie knew roller derby wasn't just a sport to Lauren; it was her life. "Coach Ritter was *not* happy. Carmen couldn't make it either, but at least she called to say there were mechanical problems at the dry cleaners. Sharmila was late. But you being a no-show really sent Coach over the edge. She thinks no one is taking the team seriously."

"Sorry," Annie apologized again. She was good at that.

"Well, don't do it again. We need you. You're part of the team and the team needs all of its members. Especially if we want that championship."

"Trust me, I'll be there next time."

Lauren relaxed and then smiled. She wasn't the sort to stay angry for long. "Good. Because I miss you when you're not around." She gave Annie a friendly punch on the shoulder and headed off to her class.

Annie leaned back against the lockers, drained of any energy. She knew she shouldn't have done it but really, it was just one practice. It wasn't going to make a difference. And as she watched Tyler walking down the hall towards her, she knew it had been worth it.

Jeans, untucked shirt, and a cashmere jumper, he looked like a model from Abercrombie & Fitch. She felt weak at the knees as he approached. He greeted her with a quick kiss and put his arm around her waist. "Hey, babe. Going my way?"

Annie grinned, her confrontation with Lauren forgotten. "As a matter of fact I was. How did you guess?"

Tyler tapped his head. "Intuition."

The bell rang and they headed to their English class together. People passing gave them a quick hello or waved. Everyone seemed to know them. Or rather, they knew Tyler. And they all seemed eager to be considered his friends.

Except one person.

Lexie.

She had returned to the Japanese theme again, wearing a

dark blue kimono and chopsticks in her elaborate hairdo. Annie waved and gestured for Lexie to come over, but Lexie darted off to class with her friend Aaron from manga club.

Understandable, Annie reasoned. The bell had just rung. But she couldn't help suspecting that Lexie was still punishing her for what happened in Rosie Lee's, even though Annie had apologized.

The two free desks in the room were not together so Tyler left Annie in the middle and went to sit in the back with the other jocks. Ms Schwartz, their English teacher, was shuffling through her recycled bottle caps bag and didn't seem ready to start the class. Kelsey went up to Annie and sat on her desk like they were best mates.

"What do you want?" Annie asked, narrowing her eyes.

Kelsey gave Annie a smug grin. "Oh, someone's grumpy! Up late last night? I'd offer some concealer for those bags under your eyes, but I don't think I have enough. Besides, I wouldn't want your freakish germs contaminating it."

"Yes, I did have a late night, actually," Annie said. Giving Kelsey her sweetest smile, she added, "With Tyler."

With a grunt of disapproval, Kelsey slid off Annie's desk and went back to her seat just as Ms Schwartz looked up from her bag.

"Hello, class. I believe you have papers to give in." Ms Schwartz rubbed her hands as if Christmas had come early. For her. Everyone else, including Annie, grumbled at having to hand in their essays.

Annie sneaked a look at Tyler. He didn't look nearly as tired as she felt and he didn't seem worried either. She wondered if he had even finished his paper last night. Hopefully he had. She couldn't stand the idea of him failing and getting kicked off the soccer team because of her.

Grades seemed to be on other people's minds as well. At lunch, Annie almost crashed into Liz. The Liberty Belles' captain had an apple in her mouth while marking a textbook with her finger and trying to pay for a sandwich.

"Do you need help?" Annie asked.

Liz shook her head as she handed crumpled notes over to the cashier. "No hank you. Ah haf to go hudy." She put her wallet and sandwich in her open bag and took the apple out of her mouth. "All the colleges will be looking at this semester's GPA to decide whether I get in. I'll catch you later."

"Good luck," Annie said. Liz lifted the arm holding the textbook in acknowledgement as she headed to the computer lab. Annie was only just starting to understand Grade Point Averages. She knew a 4.0 was the highest GPA only because that was Carmen's derby number and she got straight As. Other than that, the system still confused her.

The way colleges here accepted students was so different from England. Back home, university acceptance was conditional based on A-level results, tests taken at the end of their last school year. Annie remembered the older girls at school anxiously awaiting their results, which didn't come until August, to find out what university they would go to. She thought it was weird that colleges here accepted students months before they had finished high school and got their final marks.

Annie scanned the cafeteria and found Lexie at a table in the back focusing more on her sketchbook than her lunch. Not that Annie could blame her. The cafeteria was not known for its fine cuisine.

"*Konichiwa*," Annie said as she set her bag down next to Lexie. "You're all by yourself."

Lexie looked up from her drawing, a variation of the famous painting "The Scream" but with a brown-skinned girl with wild ringlets instead of a ghoulish guy. From Lexie's MP3 player, Annie could hear the distinct throaty voice of Siouxsie and the Banshees. Lexie set down her brown pencil and gave Annie a small smile. "I guess I just wanted to work on this piece."

"It's looking amaz—" Annie started to compliment her before she got interrupted by a voice booming across the cafeteria.

"Yo, Ann-nie!" Tyler stood in the middle of the crowded room surrounded by his teammates, beckoning her to his table. "We're over here."

Annie held up a hand to indicate she'd be there in a minute. When she turned back to her friend, Lexie had raised the volume of her music and picked up her pencil to shade in the girl's hands.

"Why don't we go and sit with them?" Annie suggested.

Lexie kept her eyes on the drawing. "I don't feel like it."

"I know Tyler's said some things that came out wrong, but he's really funny and sweet. If you got to know him better…"

"No, thanks."

Annie glanced from the soccer players back to her best friend. Maybe if she tried a different tactic… "You know, Javier is a great footballer. He's really nice and cute, too. And apparently he writes poetry. I don't think he's seeing anyone."

"He's gay," Lexie muttered.

"Is he?" Annie turned back to the table. The possibility had never even occurred to her. Not that it changed anything. He was still the guy on the team she liked the best. After Tyler, of course.

Lexie made a noise in the back of her throat as she switched from the brown to the blue pencil. "That's what he told me when I asked him out last May."

So Lexie DID fancy him. At least I'm on the right track. Annie wasn't going to give up. She searched the other guys at the soccer table. Jackson, Aidan, Sergei, and Ricky were all taken. She didn't really know Cameron, but Tyler seemed to think he was a bit of an idiot. Ethan, Hasan, and Ezekiel weren't artsy in the least, so they probably wouldn't have anything in common with Lexie. But now that the idea had crossed Annie's mind, she was determined. Lexie needed a boyfriend. If Lexie was dating someone as well, she wouldn't mind Annie spending time with Tyler.

"How about Damien? Have you seen the leather armband he made? It's really cool."

Lexie scrunched up her nose. "Eww, no. He's my cousin."

"He can't be." Annie spoke without thinking how that sounded. She hadn't meant to be rude, but Damien was Native American.

"All right, step-cousin or whatever. Anyway, in my mind, we're related."

Annie sighed. "Well, who DO you fancy?"

Lexie finally put her pencils down and stared at Annie. "Look, don't get me wrong. I like boys, but I don't need one to make me happy."

Annie frowned. She certainly didn't *need* a boyfriend, but she loved having one.

She looked across the cafeteria again and caught Tyler's eye. He jerked his head towards his friends and gave her a puzzled look that asked why she wasn't joining them. She didn't know what to do. Lexie had gone back to her sketch. Why was Lexie forcing her to choose? If she was going to ignore Annie, then there was no point in staying, right?

"Do you mind if I go and sit with them?"

Lexie didn't say anything, just kept drawing.

"I'll stay if you want me to," Annie said.

There was still no response from Lexie. Annie shrugged, picked up the sandwich she hadn't even started and headed to the table where Tyler sat with his teammates. It was difficult to tell with all the noise in the cafeteria, but she was pretty sure she heard Lexie mutter, "*Sayonara.*"

Maybe she should go back to her friend … except Tyler had seen her coming and was making room for her at the table. He gave her his heart-breaking smile as she slid in next to him.

"Hey, Annie." Javier nodded when she sat down.

"Hiya," Annie said.

Tyler put an arm around her and leaned over to whisper in her ear. "I was getting lonely without you."

"Me too," Annie said automatically as she unwrapped the sandwich she'd brought from home: chunky peanut butter and strawberry jam.

Tyler kept the arm around her as he turned back to his team. "Did I tell you? Coach said a scout from Illinois College was at our last game."

"Dude, do they give free rides?" Ethan asked.

"What kind of grades do they want?" Damien wondered.

"Do you think they'll send scouts again in a couple years?" Javier turned his attention to Tyler.

The soccer players continued to fire off questions. Annie looked for opportunities to say something, anything, but what did she know about American colleges? She was only in ninth grade. There wasn't anything she could contribute to the conversation; she didn't know which schools had the good teams. She didn't even know whether a free ride had anything to do with transport. Every once in a while, Tyler would give her shoulder a squeeze, reminding her that he hadn't forgotten she was there. Over in the corner, Lexie had been joined by her friend Aaron, who had dyed black hair and a nose ring, and his equally cool-looking girlfriend, Becky. They were all studying something in Lexie's sketchpad. *I guess she didn't really want to be alone*, thought Annie.

At another table, Annie caught Holly, Sharmila, Jesse, and some other kids laughing as they ate their lunches. Holly was laughing so hard she spat out some of her drink, making everyone laugh even harder. They all looked like they were having so much fun that Annie couldn't help wishing she knew what the joke was.

Leaning more into Tyler's shoulder, she did everything to focus on the conversation at her table. Soccer. That's all they ever talked about. OK, so she and Dad had enjoyed going to a few Chelsea matches back home but it had never mattered that much whether their team won or not. To these boys, soccer was the only thing that mattered – even now that the season was over.

Annie finished her sandwich in silence and nursed her water bottle just to have something to do. Who knew being popular could feel so lonely.

Chapter Seven

Saturday night was roller derby bout night.

Tyler had mentioned going to the movies but there was no way Annie was going to miss the bout. If the Liberty Belles won this one, they would be competing for the league championship in December. If they didn't win, well, at least they weren't out of the running yet.

Annie got to the rink early, ready to show Coach Ritter that she wasn't skiving off this time. Her skates were on the counter, waiting for her, when she got to Jesse's rental booth.

He brushed the hair out of his eyes and beamed when he saw her. "Hey, I was worried when you didn't show last practice. Ankle holding up?"

"Yeah, sorry about that." Annie grabbed her skates, avoiding his eyes. There was no way she would say what she had really been doing that night. "Lost track of time."

"Coach Ritter was real pissed. I think you might have some grovelling to do."

Annie sighed. "Lauren told me. Did I miss anything important?"

Jesse shrugged. "I think they were working on some new plays, but I don't know what they were."

Crumbs. Just what Annie needed, everyone on the team knowing what to do except her. Well, at least Carmen hadn't made it to practice either so maybe the two of them could pick up the plays together. "Thanks. I got here early to make up what I missed."

"Good luck – but try to think of a better excuse than losing track of time. If you want my advice, start kissing up now." He jerked his head in Coach's direction and then turned to organize the rack of skates behind him.

Annie turned. Her stomach tightened into a massive knot. Sure enough, there was Coach Ritter skating over the faded carpet towards her. Her auburn hair was pulled into two messy buns on the top of her head. But instead of looking pretty, the hairdo looked menacing. Probably because of the deep scowl etched into Coach's face.

Jesse was right. Better start apologizing now before she felt really sick.

"I'm really sorry I missed practice. It's just with homework and helping Dad at Rosie Lee's..." Annie trailed off. Dad and

Coach Ritter were friends. She didn't know how often they talked, but the last thing she wanted was for Coach to catch her lying. Better stick with the kissing up. "Anyway, I'm sorry and it'll never happen again. I'll do some extra laps to warm up and will stay after the bout and help clean up. I can—"

"Annie, stop." Coach Ritter stared at her with arms crossed. "Sit."

Annie plopped down on the bench and took a deep breath. Coach sat down next to her. Annie let out her breath. Oh, thank goodness. Coach didn't seem like she was going to scream at her.

A second later, Annie wished she was being screamed at. The disappointment in Coach Ritter's voice was much worse. "I don't know what to say to you. You don't even have a valid reason for not showing up. And you didn't even call. I thought you knew better than that. That you took the sport and this team seriously." Coach Ritter shook her head in disbelief.

Annie started to say something, anything, in her defence, but Coach continued before any words came out. "You're a great athlete, one of the most promising on the team. I can see you playing in an All-Star league one day. It's one thing to miss practice for a good reason, we all have things that come up, but you should have let me know as soon as possible."

"I—" Annie started to say it was an accident but Coach wasn't going to be interrupted.

"I know you weren't at Rosie Lee's. I stopped for a muffin before coming here and would have driven you over but your dad said you were with a friend."

From the way she said "friend" Annie knew Coach knew what kind of "friend" Tyler was, and wasn't impressed.

"I'm sorry, it's just—"

"I don't want to hear it. You let me down, and you let your team down. If you want to remain a Liberty Belle, don't let that happen again."

"Yes, Coach." Annie stared at her clenched hands. *Don't cry*, she told herself. *Don't cry*.

"Now, take those skates back to Jesse. You won't be needing them today."

Annie looked up in horror. Any thought of crying was gone. "What?"

Coach Ritter stood up. "I've taken you off the roster for today. You can still be an NSO if you like."

"You can't do that. That's out of order!"

"No, it's not. Girls who don't take the team seriously don't play. I suggest you apologize to your teammates, and then you can help keep score."

Coach Ritter skated away and started calling out warm-ups for the girls on the rink. Carmen, who had also missed the last practice, was still allowed to play. Just because she had a stupid work emergency excuse. It wasn't fair.

Annie kicked the bench in frustration. Last month she had been a non-skating official because she had a sprained ankle. But to be demoted to an NSO now was insulting and unnecessary. One practice. One measly, stupid, little practice and she couldn't play today. So unfair. If she'd known this would happen, she wouldn't have bothered showing up. She could have been at the movies with Tyler instead of being subjected to such humiliation.

Maybe she should go. Ring Tyler up right now, get him to pick her up, and take her away.

No, then Coach Ritter would kick her off the team for sure. *"If you want to remain a Liberty Belle,"* echoed in her mind. Not that being off the team would be such a bad thing, if this was how she was going to get treated. Still, if she wasn't going to play roller derby any more, she wanted it to be because *she* quit, not because she'd been kicked out.

With an internal grumble, Annie picked up the skates and dumped them on the counter in front of Jesse.

"Looks like I'll be keeping score today." She rolled her eyes, not explaining what was going on. He must have known; he did try to warn her. "So unfair. One practice is not the same as missing a bout. She knows I'm trustworthy; I babysit her kids."

"I was afraid of that. Coach Ritter doesn't make exceptions for anyone." He gave her a sympathetic look before reaching under the counter and tossing her a black and white ref's shirt. Annie sighed. On the back it had her derby name, Anne R. Key. She had got the idea from the song, "Anarchy in the UK", by one of her favourite punk groups, the Sex Pistols. Jesse had put her derby name on the shirt with black tape last month when she couldn't skate. She didn't know whether to be pleased or sad that he hadn't removed it.

"Cheers." She pulled the shirt over her head. It clashed horribly with her gold hot pants and purple tights.

Jesse pointed to the easel set up on the rink. "Board's all ready for you. Let me know if you need anything. A song or something to cheer you up." With that he pressed a button on the sound system and on came the Beastie Boys' "(You Gotta) Fight for Your Right (To Party)".

Annie smiled. Almost. Whatever else was going on, at least Jesse was a good friend.

She walked into the rink towards her whiteboard. The derby track ovals were painted onto the rink's floor, but there was still plenty of room out of bounds for officials and players. Annie's scoreboard was just behind the jammers' line, next to one of the team's benches. In some bouts, like the first one Annie went to, audience members could sit right on the rink floor, but here spectators sat on the bleachers on the opposite side of the starting lines for optimal viewing.

"Benched you, huh? Guess you're not such a princess," Holly smirked as she skated towards Annie, turned backward and got on her toe brakes for a perfect tomahawk stop. Annie braced herself for the worst. Holly would have to rub it in. It was in her nature. "Yeah, that's never happened to me. I've never bailed on my team. Not for a guy at least. But for a Lady Gaga concert in Chicago? Totally worth it."

Holly winked. New admiration and respect for Annie appeared on Holly's face as if they were now partners in crime. The older girl skated off on one skate and changed direction to face Annie while still on that skate. "Third row seats!" she mouthed and held out three fingers.

Annie's first real smile of the night crept onto her face. It was nice having Holly on her side, as if Holly suddenly admired Annie for being a bit of a rebel. Annie took a deep breath and headed over to the rest of the team. Now was the time, a minute before the bout started.

"I'm really sorry for skiving off the other day, guys." Annie looked at each of the girls in turn. "And I'm really, really sorry that because of it, I can't play today."

Liz gave her a hug. With Liz on skates, the two were the same height. "I know, sweetie. We all make mistakes. The important thing is that you're still here and you're one of us."

The other girls nodded in agreement and headed to the bench as Jesse turned on the PA system to announce the start of the bout and introduce the members from each team.

Looking like he'd been in a fight with a bag of flour and lost, Dad came rushing into the rink. He'd always made every single event of Annie's, whether gymnastics, school-related, or roller derby. Annie loved him for that, but for the first time wished he hadn't come. He glanced at the girls lined up by the benches. Each team was on either side of the chairs making up the penalty box. Annie could tell from his frown that he didn't see her and was panicking. Reluctantly, she lifted a hand and waved for his attention. It took him a second to spot her away from the team. His expression changed from worry to surprise.

"Beanie," he said. He had started calling her String Bean, or Beanie, after she grew a foot last year and became too tall for gymnastics. "Are you OK? Have you hurt your ankle again?"

Annie looked at the track. The opposing team, the Prairie Girls, were still skating around. "Coach Ritter pulled me from the bout because I missed practice on Thursday. I know, I'm sorry, and I'll never do it again."

Dad sighed, running a hand through his hair which made it stick straight up. "In that case, I'm going back to Rosie Lee's. I still need to make five kinds of cookie dough. I'll pick you up at the end and we'll talk about this then."

Annie nodded and watched him leave. Usually he helped out at the bouts as an NSO, but maybe he thought she'd taken his place. It was probably for the best that he had left. She just hoped his "talk" didn't lead to another embarrassing discussion about avoiding pregnancy when all she and Tyler were doing was snogging.

She glanced around at the spectators. That was odd. Lexie wasn't there. Lexie, like Dad, had always come to watch the Liberty Belles' bouts. Probably because roller derby was the only sport she thought was cool. OK, so there were still some ruffled feathers between them, but Annie didn't think that would keep her from watching the bout. If Lexie were here, she would have given Annie a much-needed hug. Or at least she would have before Annie started going out with Tyler. Lexie had been acting so weird lately it was hard to figure her out.

Annie let out a slow breath and grabbed the black dry erase marker with one hand and the rag to wipe the board clean with the other. She was ready to keep score. The bout only lasted for two thirty-minute periods. She could stand the humiliation of being benched for that long.

Annie's humiliation was shared by her teammates when the bout started. The Prairie Girls were currently at the bottom of the league, but still managed to outplay the Liberty Belles in almost every single jam. After twenty minutes of the first period, the Belles were lagging by eighteen points. Not a huge gap, but embarrassing enough to really bother Annie.

If only Coach would let me lace up my skates. I could help the Belles catch up.

No such luck. At least not for the Belles.

"Jammer Holly Terror gets sent to the penalty box for elbowing Crossing Jordan," Jesse spoke quickly. "Which puts the Prairie Girls into a power jam!"

No!

Annie wanted to cover her eyes in horror. Holly said a few choice words on her way to the box. Not that it helped. For the one minute Holly was in the box, the Belles would be without a jammer, unable to score points or call off the jam.

Lauren, Sharmila, Tashi, and Liz, tried to hold the Prairie Girls' jammer, Guard-a-Lupe, back. Tried. Liz accidentally stuck out her skate and got sent to the box for low blocking. Guard-a-Lupe, a tall and heavy girl built like a bull, barged her way through the pack and raced back around to do it again. And again. When the ref finally blew the whistle indicating the end of that jam, the Prairie Girls had racked up fifteen more points.

Annie wiped the old score off. With a heavy heart, she sighed and wrote the new score: "32 Belles – 65 Prairie Girls".

After the halftime break, things didn't get better. Holly, Liz, Sharmila, and Natalia all scored some points during their turns as jammer, but so did the Prairie Girls. Instead of screaming at her team, Coach Ritter wore the same look of disappointment she'd had earlier with Annie.

"Focus, girls, focus. Watch those gaps. Remember those plays we've been working on." Coach Ritter clapped encouragement.

"Guard-a-Lupe is back as the Prairie Girls' jammer and jamming for the Liberty Belles, we have Sharrrrmilaaaaa the Hun!" Jesse announced while Annie clapped her hands unenthusiastically. Jesse didn't have to make it so obvious that he liked Sharmila. *He's probably imagining her in a pink and gold sari,* Annie thought sulkily.

"Sharmila the Hun breaks through the pack first, and yes! She's your lead jamm-merrr! What a move. She rounds the corner, closing in on the pack again. Guard-a-Lupe is still trying to get through the pack but the Belles are standing firm. Sack 'n' Jill gets sent to the box for grabbing Lauren Disorder. Sharmila the Hun squeezes through a gap in the pack, passing Guard-a-Lupe for a graaaand slaaaaaam! And the Liberty Belles are back in the running!"

Annie jumped up and down, cheering as loudly as she could. She wasn't actually supposed to show favouritism as the scorekeeper, but at this stage she didn't care. Sharmila scored a total of nine points – earning an extra point for passing the opposing jammer – and the Prairie Girls none, before she called off the jam. Even though Sharmila's points didn't even up the score, it was still a great play. The Liberty Belles were back in the game.

Except the Prairie Girls weren't surrendering. No one scored in the next jam. In the jam after that, both teams scored a handful of points. Not that it helped. The opposing team was still leading.

Annie alternated between watching the girls in the rink and the clock. The nails on her left hand were bitten to the quick. The Belles *could* still win. Sixteen points behind wasn't too much. A power jam in their favour could square things right up…

But it wasn't going to happen. Not today.

The Prairie Girls were playing uncharacteristically well and the Belles kept getting penalties. When the buzzer sounded the end of the bout, Annie grumbled as she wrote the final score on the board: "89 Belles – 102 Prairie Girls". The Belles' first loss of the season. She felt worse than she had when Coach Ritter had scolded her earlier. Who knew whether the Belles would have still lost if Annie had been allowed to play, but at least she wouldn't have this gnawing guilt in her stomach for not being there for them. Setting down the marker, she shuffled over to her teammates with a promise that next time they'd get the Prairie Girls back.

Forget about quitting roller derby. That wasn't even an option. Annie didn't care if Coach Ritter decided she had been too easy on Annie and wanted to keep her as an NSO for the rest of the season. She loved the sport, and her teammates, way too much not to take it seriously. She was going to work harder to prove that she had what it took to be a good teammate; she'd make sure the Belles made it to the championship bout. And won.

The next bout's opposing team had better be prepared. Anne R. Key was not going down without a fight.

Chapter Eight

The Liberty Belles' defeat brought Annie to two conclusions: the Belles were not invincible and she was never ever, *ever*, going to let her team down again. If they got defeated again, they'd do it as a team.

To help in both regards, Annie had come up with a new training regime. Yes she was fit, but she had been even fitter in her gymnastics prime. It was time to get that back. And the best part was that she had convinced Tyler to join her for the workout. At least for today. It was the most perfect plan.

Except that it was freezing on the school's track where they agreed to meet after school. Annie got there first and immediately started stretching and warming up. Tyler showed up seven minutes later, his cheeks a deep red from the cold.

"Hiya. Better start warming up." Annie leaned over to give Tyler a quick kiss. He tried to wrap his arms around her for a deeper snog, but she shook her finger. "No. You, young man, will have to wait. We've got too much to do before that."

"Remind me why we're here? Soccer season's over," Tyler grumbled as he began jogging on the spot to warm up.

"We need the training." Annie stretched an arm over her head.

"Speak for yourself. I'm in perfect shape."

Annie grinned. "Yeah? Then this should be easy-peasy for you."

Tyler pulled up the zipper of his coat the remaining five centimetres. "Just 'cause I can do it, doesn't mean I want to. I checked the thermometer in the car; it's twenty-two degrees!"

"What's that in Celsius?" Annie asked as she did twenty star jumps.

"Bloody cold!" Tyler said in a fake English accent as he blew into his hands.

Annie ignored the chill. She had on her pink wool hat and matching mittens that her nana in Surrey had knitted, a yellow fleece, and enough blood circulating to keep everything but the tip of her nose toasty.

"OK, shall we start with a circuit, doing everything for a minute and resting for thirty seconds?" Annie pulled out a page she'd printed from a fitness site online and consulted it. "Let's start out with burpees."

Tyler let out a loud fake burp. When Annie gave him a

disapproving look, he grinned and said, "What? I thought you asked for burpees."

"Very funny," Annie said. "You know what I meant." She set down the paper, then leaped into the air with her arms up. Then she bent to her knees, jumped back into a plank, did a push up, before jumping her feet back to her hands and leaping in the air again. She placed her hands on her hips and smiled smugly. Let him admire how fit she was.

He did. He leaned over to kiss her. Annie let him for a second. OK, maybe two.

"Nope." She shifted away from him when he tried to put his arms around her. "You have to earn your smooches today. I'll tell you the rest of the exercises just before we do them. If they're really hard for you, I'll let you take extra breaks."

Tyler gave her a dirty look and Annie grinned back. She had no doubt that Tyler could do everything on the sheet – he didn't get his fit body by watching television all day long – but she liked teasing him about being the fitter one.

They went through the training circuit, pausing only to position themselves for the next exercise. Once they'd had finished it, Tyler was definitely panting hard. Annie sipped some water, feeling a bit tired but not exhausted.

"I still don't get what's the point in all this. We could have just as easily worked out in the gym. Or gone swimming at my parents' sports club. I bet you look hot in a swimsuit." He raised his eyebrow at her, but his charm was not going to work today. Annie had never been a quitter.

"True, but if you train in the cold, when the air is thinner, it builds stamina. I want to get super fit for derby," she said as she continued with some arm rotations. She hadn't told him about being put as an NSO during the last bout. She still felt bad about her disgrace and she didn't want him to think she blamed him when it was her fault. She should have stayed strong and insisted on going to the practice. All he knew was that the team had lost and she was determined not to let it happen again.

"It's cute how you're so into roller derby. Even if it's not a real sport."

Annie put her hands on her hips and stood straight, towering the full inch above him. "Pardon? Just because there's no ball, doesn't make it less of a sport."

Tyler took a step back so their height difference wasn't so evident. "Ah, c'mon. It's just a bunch of girls in fishnets knocking each other down."

Annie bit back a retort. Roller derby was so much more than girls in fishnets. Tyler should know that, he'd been to their bouts – well, one of them. But she didn't want to get into an argument with him. She didn't want to become like her parents. "It still requires a lot of training. Try skating a couple of jams in a row and you'll be tired."

"But it's not like it's in the Olympics," he smirked.

She could let the previous comment slide, but not this one. "Actually, Liz was telling us that it's being considered for the 2020 Olympics. If it gets approved, I'll be doing everything I can to get on that team."

As soon as Liz had mentioned it, Annie knew that was her ultimate goal. The only question in Annie's mind (and she was glad she didn't have to decide yet) was whether she'd compete for the UK or the US team.

Tyler rolled his eyes. "2020 is still ages away, and as you said, it hasn't been approved."

"Yet," Annie pointed out.

Tyler finally seemed to realize he wasn't going to win the argument so he changed the subject. "It's a shame you gave up cheerleading. That would have kept you fit, probably even more than roller skating. Maybe if you talked to Kelsey—"

Annie shook her head. There hadn't been a single moment she had regretted her choice. "No. I love roller derby. I'm not giving it up. Just like you wouldn't give up soccer. Right?"

"I guess." Tyler plopped down next to his bag.

Annie ran a hand down his chilly cheek. "Good. 'Cause we're not done here. Do you know what fartleks are?"

"The little farts that slip out when you're exercising?"

Annie laughed. "No, silly. They're—"

Tyler rolled his eyes. "Course I know what they are. Coach makes us do them. During *summer* training."

It wasn't really *that* cold, not as long as you kept moving. "Right, so let's sprint to the eighth mile marker, walk to the next, then sprint again, and so on, all the way around the track. Bet I can beat you."

He pushed himself back up to standing and gave her a cocky grin. "Yeah, right. And what do I get *when* I win?"

Hmm, finally some good motivation. She should have thought of challenging him earlier. "We stop training and you have the satisfaction of knowing you're fitter than me."

"I am fitter than you," he said in an exasperated tone as if it were a fact everyone knew.

Annie grinned. She had got him now. "Then prove it. On your marks."

They jogged over to the starting line on the track and crouched down behind it.

"Get set."

Tyler turned to look at her, his green eyes shining as he winked at her, his smile turning up slowly in a way that normally made her heart stop. Annie smiled back sweetly. She knew what he was doing, and usually it would have worked. But today her competitive streak had kicked in and she wasn't going to get easily distracted.

"Go!"

They took off at a sprint, white puffs coming out of their mouths as their warm breath hit the cold air. Tyler was thirty centimetres in front of Annie. She closed the gap to fifteen just as they switched to walking. They walked side by side but when they got to the next marker, Annie took the lead with her sprint. When she switched back to walking, Tyler wasn't at her side. She could hear him behind her, but she didn't turn around to see how close he was. If his footsteps got nearer, she'd up her speed. By the last sprint, she couldn't even hear him behind her any more. Dropping to a walk for the last portion, she finally checked to see how far behind he was. Pretty far. He wasn't even bothering to run.

His grumpy scowl was visible even from a distance as he kicked the dirt under his feet.

Annie reached a hand out to him. She didn't have the heart to rub in her victory. "You all right?"

Tyler rammed his hands into his coat pockets, shaking off her hand. "No. I'm cold and this sucks. Can we just go to my place and warm up there?"

Annie checked the time on her phone. "I was planning to train for another half an hour."

"Well, I'm leaving. So if you want a ride, it's now or never."

Annie kissed him on his flushed cheek. The fartlek had energized her instead of making her tired. "I'll run home. Catch you later."

He let out a grumble and didn't return the kiss, just shuffled away to his red sports car.

True to her word, Annie ran another lap around the track and then jogged towards her house. *Her* house. She couldn't remember when she started to think of it as hers instead of her grandparents'. Sure they had lived in Florida as long as Annie could remember, but they'd kept the Illinois house as a holiday rental until Dad and Annie moved in. Now there was no doubt that it was home. Her home.

But then there was still the flat in London. *Her* flat. The one she had grown up in and had lived in her whole life. She didn't – *couldn't* – think of it as just Mum's flat now, even though her mother was the only one living there.

Mum. She'd be here soon. Since Mum became a partner at the law firm, she hadn't taken a holiday without her Blackberry. Annie doubted that crossing an ocean would make a difference to Mum's work addiction.

And then there was the question of her and Dad. Together again. In the same house.

I hope they both behave. So many things could happen. Mum could be kind and sympathetic, but she could also be very critical – especially of Dad. As soon as Dad decided to move back to Illinois, and Annie chose to go with him, the tension between her parents had been so awkward. Mum and Dad had made such an effort not to shout or complain about the other that the air in the flat had been almost stifling. Not that having them argue was any better. Now, several months later, maybe they'd had the time they needed to cool off and appreciate each other.

Maybe if Annie could get them to spend some time alone together… She could get her friends to help her come up with a plan. Lexie was always good for creative solutions! Something that involved locking her parents up (ideally without their phones) until they realized they couldn't live without each other.

Annie sighed. It was an entertaining idea that would only work in a cheesy romantic comedy. Still, if there was something that would get them back together…

She passed houses with their Thanksgiving decorations and brown, gold, and red leaves scattered across the lawns. The people of Liberty Heights loved to have an excuse to decorate their homes. The decorations weren't as elaborate and plentiful as they had been for Halloween, but still pumpkins and squashes of various colours and shapes were on display on the front porches, a couple of scarecrows and pilgrims adorned the gardens, and one house had a large inflatable turkey that bobbed its head in the breeze as she jogged by.

There was nothing like this in London. Other than Christmas decorations, and an occasional garden gnome, people didn't normally dress up their houses in England.

Not that London wasn't already beautiful, with its old-fashioned streets and posh terraced houses. Their flat was right on a leafy, green square, not far from a tube station that would take her anywhere she wanted to go in the city. She missed that, definitely.

As she drew to a stop outside her house, Annie suddenly felt unsure where she belonged. Both Liberty Heights and London were "home". But she couldn't be in two places at the same time. Annie shivered, suddenly aware of the cold Tyler had complained about.

Chapter Nine

The school bell rang at midday on Tuesday, leading to an even louder than normal stampede of students rushing to get out. And that was with a lot of kids already gone for the holidays. Kelsey had mentioned last week (several times, very loudly) that her parents were taking her to the Bahamas for Thanksgiving. Good riddance, as far as Annie was concerned.

As she pushed and shoved her way towards the school door, she wondered why the district had bothered with classes at all. The day and a half of school this week had been pointless. She knew she wasn't the only one who hadn't taken in anything the teachers had said.

Besides, she had far more pressing things to do than school. Mum was arriving today. In fact, she'd be landing in Chicago really soon and would take the two-hour shuttle bus to Liberty Heights. Which meant Annie had a lot of work to do before then. The last thing she wanted was for Mum to start criticizing the house as soon as she walked in. And with good reason; the house was a tip.

One of the first rooms Mum would see when she walked in would be the kitchen. Better start there. Although really, when Annie saw the state it was in, she wondered whether they should have taken up Grandma and Gramps' offer to go on a cruise with them for Thanksgiving instead. It would certainly have been easier than sorting out this huge mess.

Dad had made Mum's favourite orange-cranberry muffins before leaving that morning to open up at Rosie Lee's. The muffins were the perfect combination of tangy and sweet, but Dad clearly hadn't had time to clear up the chaos he'd caused.

The sink was piled high with breakfast dishes, measuring cups, a mixing bowl, beaters, spatulas, and the muffin tin. There were also halved oranges crusting on the counter and a bag of dried cranberries spilling onto the floor. The only thing Dad seemed to have cleaned was his favourite, and highly expensive, chef's knife.

Great, Dad, thanks for the help.

Not that it was exactly his fault. He mentioned at breakfast that he had thirty-six specially ordered pies to bake: pumpkin, pecan, apple, and one chocolate-pear pie for an old dear who begged him to make it just like her great-nana had in the seventeen hundreds or something.

Well, no point staring at the mess. It wasn't going to improve unless she cracked on. She changed into some scruffy clothes (she'd been wearing a nice jumper and a short skirt over tights, which had made Tyler whistle at the sight of her long legs!). Then she turned on Aerosmith's "Dude (Looks Like a Lady)" because it reminded her of when Robin Williams was cleaning in drag while pretending to be Mrs Doubtfire.

She got the dishes loaded into the dishwasher, wiped down the counters, and tested one of Dad's muffins. It was fabulous. But even with her efforts, the kitchen still looked anything but fabulous: it was old-fashioned and worn, and the decor hadn't been changed since the 1980s, she guessed. At least Dad had removed the lace curtains that were in the windows when they first moved in. And it was clean now.

She shoved the tea towels into the wash and went to gather any clothes she could find on the floor. There were loads from both hers and Dad's rooms. It was so much easier to throw things on the floor than put them back where they belonged. Especially now that Annie was taking more time to look nice in the mornings.

Clothes stuffed into the wash, she looked at the clock. There was at least an hour before Mum arrived. Maybe more if her flight was late or the immigration queue was long.

Annie swept, mopped and vacuumed the whole house before tackling the bathroom Mum would share with her. Dad's bathroom would have to be left to fester – neither she nor Mum would dare venture there.

The room Mum would be staying in had been Dad's while

he was growing up. Grandma always told the story of attacking the room with six coats of paint to cover the black walls when she and Gramps decided to move to Florida fifteen years ago and turn the house into a rental. Now it was yellow, flowery, and looked like a "grandma" room. Oh well, Mum would no doubt think it was an improvement over the heavy metal posters that had offended her on her last visit here.

Annie changed the sheets, set out some fresh towels, and arranged a small bouquet she had bought yesterday after roller derby practice. She knew Mum would appreciate it. Mum always said flowers brightened up any room.

Now it was time to deal with her own room. Groan. Mum would not respect her privacy and stay out. Almost every time they Skyped, Mum mentioned the state of the room. And that was looking at it through a webcam. In person, she might have a whole lot more to say about its tidiness. Or lack thereof.

After making her bed, organizing her desk seemed to be the next logical step. She found the essay she had written on *The Taming of the Shrew* the day she and Tyler should have been studying. The grade was still the same as it had been when Ms Schwartz returned it to her: C+ with a sad face.

"Not your best effort," the English teacher had written. Annie shoved it in the bottom of a drawer. No way was she going to leave that around for Mum to spot. Especially since the essay before that one got an A.

Tyler hadn't told her his mark for his essay but he was still on the soccer team so he must have scraped by.

Going through the papers strewn across the desk, Annie noticed a black smudge on her finger. She slumped into her chair as she pulled out what had caused it: a charcoal caricature of herself in full derby gear. Two long brown pigtails trailed behind her, partially covering the derby number inked on her arm like a tattoo: "5'11"½", a reference to her height. On the cartoon Annie's shirt was the Sex Pistols' "God Save the Queen". The Annie on the paper had a look about her that said she could conquer the world. Lexie had given it to her shortly after her first bout.

Annie smoothed out one of the corners. She wished she was feeling as confident as her cartoon alter ego looked; maybe the cartoon Annie could tell the real Annie how to win over the artist who had drawn it. She couldn't remember the last time she and Lexie had said anything more than a "hi" in passing. Annie knew she'd let herself get distracted by Tyler, but she didn't think she should take all the blame. Lexie was being overly sensitive. Still, it was strange not walking to school with her any more. Annie got a pin and stuck the brilliant drawing on the wall. She really should ring Lexie. But the last few times she'd tried, it had gone to voicemail, and Lexie hadn't returned her calls.

Ding-dong!

The doorbell. Mum! Annie shovelled the rest of the things from her desk into a drawer and raced to open the door.

There was Mum. Philippa Bradley was wearing smart brown boots under wide-leg tan trousers, with a salmon-coloured silk blouse open at the collar showing a string of pearls, all under a knee-length white wool coat. Her shoulder-length brown hair was perfectly styled with the ends curled up. Mum looked as if she had just strolled in from a posh meeting in Chicago instead of off a long ride on an aeroplane.

"Annie, sweetheart."

"Mum!" Annie rushed into her mother's arms.

Mum held Annie for a second before extending her arms and peering through her glasses to have a good look at her. "Are you still growing?"

Annie shook her head. "I don't think so."

Mum set down her bags just inside as Annie closed the door. "Well, you certainly look grown-up. It's great to see you."

Annie grinned. "You too. Here, I'll take your bags to your room."

"I'm sorry, did I wake you?" Mum put her coat in the cupboard by the door and followed Annie with her leather computer case. "Although, if that's the state of your pyjamas, we'd better go shopping while I'm here."

Annie cursed herself for not remembering to tidy *herself* up before Mum arrived. She dumped the bags and quickly changed out of the smelly gear and into the clothes she had worn to school.

She met Mum in the hallway and led her to the kitchen. What they needed was to get back on the right footing and food always worked.

"Dad made you some muffins."

"Ah, I really shouldn't. I've been eating gluten-free since you left." Mum placed her hands on her hips. Now that she mentioned it, Mum did look a bit trimmer. Not that she needed to lose weight. Annie, after all, had got her lean shape from her. There was no way *she* was going gluten-free unless some doctor forced her to, kicking and screaming.

Annie picked up the plate and held them close to Mum so she could get a whiff of their tangy, sweet smell. "They're cranberry-orange."

"Are they?" Mum's eyes lit up for a second before they went back to their stern look as she gave in. "Better put the kettle on, then. I brought my own tea and an extra box for you too. Last time I was here the tea your grandmother served me was best thrown down the drain."

Typical Mum – if she gave in to one thing, she found another thing to criticize. Annie took the box of tea Mum retrieved from her room. It was in posh, triangular sachets that showed the loose leaves inside. Much nicer than anything they drank at home when Annie had lived there.

"You can get good tea here now." Annie poured the water into mugs and handed one to Mum along with a spoon and a dessert plate for a saucer, and got the milk from the fridge. "Dad keeps a box of Yorkshire Gold here but serves Twinings at the café."

Mum poured a drop of milk into her tea and reached for a muffin. "And how is that going? The business, I mean."

"Great!" Annie said a bit too enthusiastically. Last month Rosie Lee's had been struggling, but it had certainly picked up recently. "With the holidays, people are getting Dad to make their pies. The café's beginning to be a local hangout."

Mum glanced around the kitchen. "Well, let's hope he can put some money into doing up this house. It hasn't changed since I was here in the nineties."

Annie set her mug down hard, splashing some of the tea on the table. Couldn't Mum at least appreciate that it was clean? That Annie had spent hours tidying up just for her? "Do you have to criticize everything?"

Mum's eyes narrowed as she pushed her glasses up her nose. "Don't you take that tone with me, Annie. But you're right. I'm being rude. The state of this house is none of my business and I apologize."

They were silent for a few minutes until Annie asked Mum about work and things in London. They finished their tea and muffins – Mum even helped herself to another muffin, saying there was no point in trying to keep to a diet while she was here. Not with Dad's gorgeous cooking. At least there was one thing she couldn't find fault in.

Mum helped with the washing up. She set the tea towel down after washing her hands and looked around.

"I fancy getting some fresh air," Mum said. "Why don't you show me the town? All I remember is trying my first root beer float at a diner that's your father's café now. I'd love to see what he's done with it."

Annie nodded. Of course they would have to go to Rosie Lee's, there'd be no avoiding it. She just hoped Mum didn't put it down like she had the house. Annie knew her tone would be much sharper if Mum dared diss Rosie Lee's. Annie sent Dad a quick text to let him know they were on their way.

The air was crisp but not as cold as it had been on other days. Annie pointed out a few things as they walked the few blocks to downtown.

"I forgot how small it is." Mum glanced from the railway tracks with a wood behind them to the detached houses with their front and back gardens. Straight in front was the downtown area with its quaint brick buildings. Annie remembered thinking the same thing when she roller-bladed through the town on her first day, but now she was determined to stay positive.

"It is a bit small, but this way you know your neighbours." Annie smiled at a woman pushing a pram with triplets. "Hiya! How're the little poppets?"

"Great! I actually got five hours of sleep last night. A miracle. Annie, tell your dad my husband's coming tomorrow for the pies." The woman waved before crossing the street.

"Will do." Annie waved back and turned to Mum. "See? Everyone's so friendly."

Mum seemed to stiffen a bit. "I wouldn't like everyone knowing my business. There's no privacy."

Annie shrugged. "Doesn't bother me."

"And what do you do for entertainment? I don't imagine you have a theatre or any museums," Mum said, as if she had time to do things in London other than work.

"Well, there's roller derby," Annie said with a smile. "That's what I do for fun."

Mum didn't comment.

"Or we could go shopping," Annie suggested. Not that she was a huge clothes hound, but it was something she always enjoyed doing with Mum.

"Yes, that would be good," Mum nodded. "You need new pyjamas, and we should get you some new bras while we're at it. You're bursting out of that one."

"Mum!" Annie crossed her arms over her chest and looked around to see if anyone had heard. Why did Mum always have to point out the most embarrassing things? Even if they were true.

Mum smiled and patted Annie's shoulder. She didn't pursue the subject. Instead she changed it. "Still dating that boy?"

"Yes!" Annie gushed. Just the thought of Tyler sent shivers down her spine. Was he thinking about her right now? "He's amazing."

"Yo, Ann-nie! C'mere!"

Annie turned quickly, running a hand through her hair. As if it was fate, or destiny, or psychic powers, there he was in his car. Tyler pulled up in front of them and leaned across the passenger seat, flashing his dazzling smile. "Hell-loo, you must be Mrs Turner."

"Ms Bradley," Mum said crisply. Annie's stomach squirmed. She knew Mum had gone back to her maiden name, but it was the first time Annie had actually heard her use it. "And you are?"

Annie blushed at her mum's businesslike tone. Best to introduce them and get it over with quickly. "Mum, this is Tyler."

"Tyler?"

"Tyler Erickson," Annie added quickly. Mum believed people should always be introduced by their full names.

"It's so great to meet you." Tyler winked and smiled wider. "I can see where Annie gets her good looks. If I didn't know better, I'd say you were her older sister."

Mum raised an eyebrow. She didn't look charmed by Tyler's flattery.

She must be knackered from the flight and time difference, Annie thought. That had to be it.

"I'm going to show her Rosie Lee's. Would you like to come?" Annie asked Tyler.

He shrugged. "Not really. Are you working too?"

"I'll help Dad out if he needs a hand – he's got a lot on at the moment."

Tyler sighed and shifted the car back into gear. "What time will you be done? There's a movie we need to see."

Annie shook her head. "Not tonight. Mum's only here for a few days."

Tyler suddenly seemed to remember the woman standing next to Annie and gave them both a wide grin. "Fine. Call me when you're done. Ms Bradley, it's been a pleasure."

Mum nodded, although she still wouldn't return his smile.

Tyler revved the engine and took off down the street going double the speed limit.

Mum watched him before slowly turning to Annie and crossing her arms over her chest. "Does he always order you around like that?"

"Do you always have to be so judgmental?" Annie snapped back.

Mum gave her a hurt look. "I only want what's best for you, sweetheart."

"Then stop putting me down." As soon as the words were out of her mouth, she regretted it. But this was just like when she had to quit gymnastics when she grew too tall last year. Mum had taken it almost as badly as Annie herself. Because Philippa Bradley always wanted the best. She could never accept that her daughter wasn't.

Annie closed her eyes for a second and did a quick calculation. Mum was only here until Saturday and Annie was already trying to work out how many more hours of her mother's criticism she'd have to put up with.

Chapter Ten

As soon as the door jingled open, Dad rushed out from the kitchen with his hair sticking up in all directions and his apron covered in flour and bits of dough.

Annie held her breath. Mum was already in a mood. If Dad was stressing about the baking, he might be grumpy too.

She didn't need to worry. Dad burst into a wide smile at the sight of them. "Pippa."

"Davy." Mum smiled a real smile, and not her usual tight-lipped one.

Dad wrapped her in a tight hug and they kissed each other on the cheek. When he let go, Mum brushed the flour off her blouse but kept her smile.

"You look great," Dad said.

"As do you." Mum looked him up and down.

Annie waited for the criticism about his appearance, some comment about Dad needing a haircut or new shoes since one of his trainers was covered in paint. But instead Mum focused on the café.

There were a few people at the tables, reading newspapers, sipping tea, or trying to wipe cupcake icing off their toddler's hair.

"Well, it's certainly a vast improvement over what it was. You've really got something here." Mum turned around, nodding her head approvingly while Dad put his arm around Annie and beamed. Mum's eye caught sight of Lexie's mural and she walked from one end of the bus to the other studying the caricatures. "This is truly spectacular. I hope the artist gave you a fair price."

"It was Annie's friend Lexie who did it. I just feed her scones to keep her happy," Dad joked. Annie pulled away from Dad. If only scones would make Lexie happy now.

Mum peered into the display case at the arrangement of scones, muffins, cupcakes, cookies, and pies. It was like the Queen herself was inspecting the café. One of the customers even set down his newspaper and sat up a bit straighter. When Mum backed away from the display case, she seemed tempted to request a sample of everything. "They all look gorgeous. I'm really impressed with everything you've done here."

"Why thank you, Madame," Dad said in a deep voice as he bowed with a flourish.

Mum smiled again, another real one, while Annie let out

another breath. She still remembered hiding under her covers one night listening to Mum accusing Dad of being immature and Dad calling Mum a killjoy.

Mum walked over to Annie and this time she put an arm around her daughter. Annie was a few inches taller than her mum and wanted to slouch under her mother's arm. Not that she dared. The last thing Annie wanted was to be told off for not standing straight.

"And Annie looks great. Happy and healthy." Mum gave Annie's shoulder a little squeeze while Annie prepared herself for Mum's announcement that she needed bigger bras. It didn't come. Mum was being tactful for a change. "I'm so proud."

Annie stared at her in surprise. Mum never said anything she didn't mean so there must be some truth in it. She'd have to apologize for being snarky later. Mum had just been being Mum. That was her way.

Dad puffed his chest out like a prize rooster. "Well, with our killer gene pool, our daughter's bound to be fantastic."

Annie groaned under flushed cheeks as she shifted out from under Mum's arm. "OK, guys. I think I'd better tidy up in the kitchen so you can talk about me some more."

"I actually have to get back to my pies," Dad said. "Pippa, please sit. Annie will get you a pot of tea. Or a cappuccino. Her frothed milk is the best in town."

Mum looked like she was battling with herself as she repressed a yawn. "I don't think all the caffeine in the world will keep me awake. I'm suddenly exhausted. Could I have a lie down before dinner?"

Dad nodded. "Sure, we'll eat probably around seven, after we clean up here. You still like Chicago pizza, right?"

"It's been a while, but I'm sure I'll manage." Mum teased in the only way she knew how: with sarcasm.

Annie handed Mum the house key and caught the kiss Mum blew her. Dad looked like he expected a kiss too and for a second Mum seemed to lose her poise. She recovered by blowing another kiss at the whole café before going out of the door.

Dad let out a deep breath and clapped his hands. "Right. Back to work."

Annie put on an apron and washed her hands. The filtered coffee and decaf were running low, two tables needed wiping down and a customer came in for the three pies she had ordered.

Annie looked up from steaming milk when the door jingled the arrival of two new customers: Lexie and her mum.

The machine spat bits of hot milk into Annie's face before she turned the knob off. Focus Annie. She finished the latte and brought it to the seated customer before greeting the pair.

"Hiya," Annie said, avoiding Lexie's eye. When she did sneak a look at her friend, Lexie avoided her eye too.

Mrs Jones, oblivious to any tension, pulled Annie into a motherly hug. Blonde, petite, and with perfectly ironed pastel clothes, Mrs Jones was the complete opposite of Lexie who had today left Japanese fashion behind and was going for a Victorian gothic look, complete with a black corset, black buttoned shoes, thick make-up, and hair pulled into a tight bun under a minuscule, slightly askew top hat.

"Honey, it's so good to see you. I feel like it's been ages since you've been over. You must come to dinner soon. We miss you." Mrs Jones gave Annie another hug while Annie wished she were the one making pies instead of Dad. A glance at Lexie, and Annie knew not all of the Jones family would be happy for her to come to dinner.

"Yes, sorry. It's just that my mum's visiting from London."

"Really?" Lexie looked around the café, clearly trying to find someone who might fit Annie's description of Mum.

"She's tired and went back to the house. But she really liked your mural," Annie explained, hoping that would break the tension.

It didn't.

Lexie said nothing as Mrs Jones paid for the pumpkin pie she had ordered. "Why don't the three of you come over for dinner on Saturday?"

Annie shook her head while focusing on Lexie. Under the Goth make-up, Lexie's face remained expressionless. "Mum's leaving that night."

Mrs Jones looked like she had never heard such devastating news. "What a shame. We're heading to Indiana for a few days so no other night works."

"Sorry, it would have been lovely." Annie grabbed the pastry tongs and picked an apple-cinnamon scone from the case and held it out to Lexie. "Scone?"

Lexie's mouth twitched for a second but she still wouldn't

meet Annie's eye. "No, thank you."

"Happy Thanksgiving." Mrs Jones waved, still oblivious to the tension between the girls. "Best regards to your family."

The door closed slowly behind them, Lexie shuffling her feet in a strop as she left.

Annie sighed as she replaced the scone in the case. She guessed Dad was wrong. Scones weren't enough to keep Lexie happy. But what was? Annie tried to think back to when the trouble first started. The hot chocolate mix-up, of course. Even though Annie had apologized, Lexie had barely talked to her since then. Going to sit with Tyler in the cafeteria had been the last straw.

If she didn't want me to sit with them, she should have said something. She was busy drawing and didn't even bother pausing her music when I was there.

But when Annie thought about it, she knew that she and Lexie had been on shaky ground for weeks.

Since Tyler and I started going out.

Lexie had never liked Tyler. He was a jock and Lexie hated how they got so much attention. And Tyler hadn't exactly been Mr Friendly either. But still, why couldn't Lexie be happy for her? Tyler was her first boyfriend and this was the most exciting thing that had ever happened to her.

Could Lexie be jealous of Tyler and the time I spend with him? No, that was ridiculous. There was nothing to be jealous of. OK, so Tyler was Annie's boyfriend, but he wasn't her best friend. That was Lexie's job.

Was her job.

97

Chapter Eleven

Annie did her hair in two plaits as she sang along to Nirvana's "Come as You Are". Curly hair was not the goal this time. They were having a pre-Thanksgiving roller derby bout and plaits worked well for keeping her long hair out of her face. Not only was this her first bout since being benched, it was the first time both of her parents would watch her play. She couldn't wait for Mum to see her in action.

"All right, let's go," Annie said as she entered the kitchen.

Mum looked up and almost choked on her tea. "Good heavens! What on earth are you wearing?"

Annie looked down at her outfit: black and white chequered tights, short red skirt, and her black and red Liberty Belles' T-shirt which had Lady Liberty in derby gear on the front and

Annie's name and number on the back: "Anne R. Key, 5'11"½". In her opinion, she looked really good. "It's just my uniform."

"For what? Going to a disco?" Mum asked.

Dad shrugged. "It's what they wear."

Mum drained the rest of her tea as if to stop herself from saying anything else.

"Relax. It's part of the fun." Annie kissed her mum on the cheek. Now was not the time to remind Mum that she once wore a sexy pirate outfit to a friend's hen party. Annie was too excited to let her mother's comments bother her today.

They squeezed into Dad's beaten up white pickup truck with Annie stuck in the middle, her long legs bumping into the gear stick. Mum sniffed at the stained seats but didn't say anything. Considering Dad barely used the truck (it was easier to walk to Rosie Lee's than pay for parking), it wasn't as dirty as it could have been.

Annie expected the rink to be empty with so many people away for Thanksgiving, but instead the car park was already full of cars. Annie was glad people thought of bringing their out-of-town guests to the bout. The more publicity the sport got the better.

"Is this it?" Mum asked, hesitating as she climbed out of the pickup in front of a warehouse-type building on the outskirts of town. After coming here for months, Annie had got used to the roller rink but she remembered having a similar reaction to the building the first time she saw it. The roof looked like it had been patched several times and was rusted in some places. The outside walls were in desperate need of paint to cover the graffiti. The lights illuminating the sign "ROCKERS' ROLLER RINK" now only read "S I K".

"Yup," Annie said with a bit of pride. "My third home."

Mum hesitated. "It looks like it's infested."

Annie hid a grin. *It probably is.* She took her mum's hand and led her to the door. The last thing she wanted was for Mum to call a taxi to take her back to the house.

The inside of the rink had just as much character as the outside. The carpet was thin and faded, the plastic tables by the snack bar were chipped and stained. There was a permanent stench of sweat, stale popcorn, and disinfectant. Annie didn't notice it any more, but Mum scrunched up her nose.

Dad went to check in as an NSO with Coach Ritter while Annie took Mum to the skate rental booth to grab the quad skates Jesse always reserved for her.

"This is Jesse Mathieu," Annie introduced her friend, pleased that she remembered to say his full name. "Jesse, my mum, Philippa Bradley."

Jesse held out his hand and gave Mum's hand a solid shake. "Pleased to meet you. Have you had a good visit so far?"

"Yes, thank you," Mum said.

"I know Annie is thrilled to have you here. Both in town and at the bout," Jesse said.

Mum's friendly nod surprised Annie, especially considering how she had treated Tyler. "I honestly have no idea what to expect. It should be interesting."

Jesse grinned. "It's unlike any sport you've ever seen. Wait until you see Annie out there. She's amazing."

"Oh stop." Annie gave him a friendly shove.

Mum let down her guard a bit and smiled. "I'm looking forward to it. She talks so much about this, it'll be good to see what the fuss is about."

"There are a lot of rules and it can be hard to follow the first time." Jesse reached under the counter and handed Mum a programme. "This includes some of the basics and the team rosters. But if you have any questions, come see me at halftime and I'll explain what I can."

"Thank you. That's very kind," Mum said.

"Cheers." Annie grinned and waved before tucking the skates under an arm and walking away.

"I like him," Mum said when they were out of earshot. "He seems very nice."

"Yeah, Jesse's great," Annie said, not really paying attention. She searched the crowd but didn't see Tyler. She'd asked him to come to the bout, but he hadn't said whether he could make it or not. *Probably busy with his family*, she thought. But then Annie remembered that Tyler's grandparents and uncle weren't coming until tomorrow and they were going to eat Thanksgiving dinner at a posh restaurant instead of cooking at home. She shouldn't worry. There was still time for him to make it.

"Not bloody likely!"

Annie and Mum both jerked around to see who else in this small Illinois town had a London accent. It was a dark-haired man in his twenties wearing jeans and a flannel shirt arguing with a huge group of people in saris and kurtas that he wasn't going to be the next one to get married. Sharmila's family, no doubt.

"Annie *beti*." Sharmila's mum motioned her over. "Let me introduce my family from London. All here for my daughter Priya's wedding."

The introductions went around and Mum looked truly happy for the first time since arriving at the rink. She smiled and shook hands with everyone as if she were meeting long lost kinsmen, just because they all spoke the same "language".

"Sharmila, Annie," Liz called out from the rink. "Warm-up's in two minutes."

Annie left her mum with Sharmila's family and spotted Dad ready to keep time in his home-made funky tie-dyed shirt that displayed his NSO name, "Belles' Kitchen". She still hadn't put on her pads or skates. From the locker room, the rest of the team skated out in a streak of hot pants and fishnets. Holly had her underwear on *over* her fishnets: a skimpy pair of knickers with "SEXY BABE!" written across the bum. Only Lauren, who was opposed to anything remotely girly, had mid-thigh blue shorts over black leggings.

Annie put her gear on quickly on one of the threadbare benches and was about to join the girls in the rink when Sharmila gasped, "Annie, wait, you don't have your face on."

Along with their derby "uniform", the girls often wore make-up or face paint to add to the fun. Annie had put on regular make-up at home, but that wasn't enough for Sharmila who was wearing more glitter than a fairy princess. For Sharmila, who wanted to become a make-up artist, it was a crime to compete in a bout without something extravagant on your face. For Halloween, she and Lexie had done a great job in turning the whole team into vampires.

Lexie.

Annie didn't have to look around to know that once again her best friend wasn't there. She half-hoped Lexie would make this bout, but knew she was probably already in Indiana with her relatives. Annie could imagine her curled up in a chair with her sketchbook drawing caricatures of her family. *I really miss her.*

Sharmila dug out a container of glitter from her skate bag and rubbed two streaks from Annie's cheekbones to the corner of her eyes. "That'll have to do for now. I'll touch it up during halftime."

The two roller girls dashed onto the rink to warm up before Coach Ritter benched both of them for being tardy.

Within a few minutes, Jesse started announcing each of the skaters with their derby names and numbers. Unlike other sports, where numbers were just numbers, in roller derby they could include letters and symbols that had special meaning to the individual. And their derby names usually included a funny pun.

"No need to watch TV when you have Lauren Disorder to take you ten to the power of twenty-four!" Jesse introduced her. Lauren skated around the track with an exaggerated tough look but when she stopped, she burst into the sweetest smile. It was hard to believe the expressions came from the same girl.

"She's five foot eleven and a half without her skates, she's Anne R. Key!" Jesse roared.

Annie sped around the track at top speed. When she returned to her starting point, she slowed down just enough to feel safe to do a cartwheel. The left skate rolled out from under her as soon as she landed, but that was inevitable. Dad gave her a loud whistle while Mum's face was unreadable. Next bout, maybe Annie would try an aerial – a hands-free cartwheel.

Jesse finished introducing everyone and the girls shuffled around as the coaches told them who'd be starting off the first jam.

"Thank you all for coming to our Thanksgiving bout," Jesse said seconds before the bout started. "Anne. R. Key, this song's for you and your mom. Happy holidays!"

Annie's eyes widened at the sound of her derby name and then her face changed to a sheepish grin as she recognized the first bars of the song.

It was a change from Jesse's usual rock tunes, but Annie couldn't help blushing a little. Jesse had remembered her reluctant confession of having loved seeing the musical with Mum on her tenth birthday (Dad had flat out refused to go with them). Blaring from the speakers was ABBA's "Mamma Mia".

She glanced at the stands and could see Mum smiling and nodding her head as she sang along. Annie owed Jesse one for sure.

She sat on the bench as Liz then Holly played jammer the first two jams. Just as she was thinking that Coach Ritter was going to keep her benched for the whole bout, she called Annie out to be the jammer.

Yes!

Annie popped in her mouthguard and pulled on the helmet cover, or panty as they called it, with the star that identified her as the jammer. Next to her on the jammer line was the Derby Dolls' captain, Hell's Angelica.

The first whistle blew and Holly, Lauren, Natalia, and Carmen began blocking the Dolls. Then two short jammer whistles sounded and Annie took off. She was at the pack before the Dolls' blockers had barely made it off the line. Reaching the pack, she squatted down low and squeezed through the pack between two girls' legs. A second later, as she was rounding the corner, the jammer ref blew his whistle, pointed at her and held up his arms in an L-shape. Brilliant! By getting through the pack first, she was the lead jammer. Hell's Angelica could still score points – but only if Annie let her. The best thing about being the lead jammer was that Annie could call off the jam anytime she wanted. Ideally, after she had racked up some points.

She came up to the pack again. The Dolls were down to three blockers, Annie's friend Tessa Distressa having been sent to the penalty box. That was good news for Annie, one less girl blocking her way, and Annie would still get a point for passing Tessa in the box if she passed all of the other blockers.

No, not if. When!

Annie faked right and the smallest gap appeared between Holly and a Doll called Mo Jo. Annie pressed against Holly to get through – it was completely legal to use your own teammates as props. Had it been anyone else, squeezing through would have been almost impossible. But Holly weighed less than fifty kilos and was a former figure skater. As soon as Annie pushed against her teammate, Holly gracefully spun out of the way, and Annie was clear!

Two strides in front of her, Hell's Angelica was making her first lap around the ring. Annie crouched low and powered after her opponent. She could feel her extra training paying off. She was faster, stronger, and more determined than before. Hell's Angelica tried to increase her speed but was no match. Annie zipped by the Dolls' captain for a grand slam. Tessa Distressa was on her way back from the penalty box, but hadn't reached the pack yet. A quick glance under her arm and Annie saw Hell's Angelica a few strides behind.

Annie noticed a space on the inside of the pack ahead. It was her best bet. If she got pushed out of bounds, she'd just call off the jam. She dashed to the left. There was only about ten centimetres between Mo Jo's skate and the painted boundaries. The same width as a balance beam. Annie leaped into the air, her arms straight up and legs out in a perfect split. She glanced at the rink and landed on both skates just within the boundary. Tapping her hands on her hips, Annie called off the jam, having scored nine points before Hell's Angelica even had a chance to score one.

Lauren gave her a huge hug as they skated off the rink and Holly took a second to mimic Annie's splits with a grand jeté.

She landed smoothly and posed on her toe stops out of bounds.

"Mine was higher," Annie teased as she gulped some water on the bench.

Holly rolled her eyes. "It's not my fault. Your legs are, like, two feet longer. And I don't see anyone else here trying it."

"Yeah, 'cause the rest of us know skates are for skating, not for doing acrobatics." Lauren took some zebra-print duct tape from her bag to strap over a kneepad that was coming loose.

Annie tossed the helmet panty to Sharmila, the next jammer, before putting her arm around her derby wife. Lauren might not be an aerialist, but she was the best blocker on the team.

She looked into the crowd, hoping to catch Mum's eye. Dad gave her a quick thumbs up before turning back to the track. Mum on the other hand... Her expression certainly wasn't critical. More like horrified. Annie's shoulders slumped down. Why was it so hard to please her?

Annie sat out one jam and then went back out onto the track as a blocker. In roller derby, players continuously changed positions. That said, not everyone who played blocker was a jammer. Lauren, for instance, was such a tough blocker that she hardly ever played jammer. Although Annie loved playing jammer, she'd learned that first you had to be a good blocker – to keep the opposing team's blockers from knocking you down. Blocking had initially intimidated her, but now she knew just what to do. She sent Polly Socket out of bounds, booty blocked Mo Jo, got knocked down by Hell's Angelica, but was back on her skates in an instant and prevented Tessa Distressa from scoring.

All in a day's bout.

By the time the bout ended, Annie had only been sent to the penalty box once for an accidental high block (Holly had been sent to the box six times – one more penalty and she would have been ejected). She had scored a total of thirty-one points and had blocked the Derby Dolls loads of times. Seeing the final score – Liberty Belles 126 – Derby Dolls 90 – Annie knew she had played her part well. The whole team had. Their place in the championship bout was now secured, only their opponent was yet to be confirmed. What a bout for Mum to see!

The Liberty Belles skated their victory lap and slapped the hands of the audience members standing around the barrier. Dad was right there with all of Sharmila's family to congratulate the team but Mum was standing a few metres away. Annie waved at her and caught the start of a wave back as she skated past.

After the Derby Dolls had done their consolation lap, Annie skated over to her parents. Dad immediately wrapped her in a tight hug and kept his arm around her shoulders as Annie turned to Mum.

"So, what did you think?" Annie asked, her eyes still glowing with the win and the excitement of the bout.

Mum pressed her lips together in a straight line and pushed her glasses up her nose.

Oh no, here she goes with the criticism again. She doesn't know anything about roller derby so she'll pick on the one thing she does know about: my split. She'll say my legs were bent even if they weren't.

"It's..." Mum paused as she searched for the right word.

"Unique. Unlike anything I've ever seen."

Not a compliment, but better than a flat-out criticism. Good enough. Annie let go of Dad and gave Mum a hug. "I'm glad you were here."

"I just don't understand why everyone is in fancy dress," Mum wondered aloud. "That girl with the red hair looked like she was in her knickers."

Before Annie could defend Holly, Coach Ritter came up to them. Dad's eyes lit up and Annie couldn't blame him. Coach's auburn hair was loose from its earlier plait and flowing in pretty waves down her back.

"It's empowering. Roller derby girls don't have to conform to a certain image. They can wear what they want and still be tough. Hi, I'm Coach Susan Ritter." She held out her hand to Mum.

Mum's eyes narrowed, shifting from the coach to Dad and back to Coach Ritter. Her eyes landed on the coach's Celtic-style banded tattoo around her left bicep and then to Coach's low-slung jeans revealing her narrow waist and part of a much larger tattoo by her hip. When Mum finally took Coach Ritter's hand it was as if she was afraid of catching germs from it.

"I am Annie's mother," Mum said briskly, without offering her own name. "Do you, uh, play this game too?"

"I retired from the sport a few years ago. Shoulder injury." Coach Ritter didn't seem to be picking up on Mum's cold vibes as she smiled sadly and rotated her shoulder.

"But Susan here is a nurse, and a mom. She'd never put the

girls in danger," Dad quickly added, putting a friendly hand on the coach's shoulder.

"I see," Mum said, staring at Dad's lingering hand.

There was a tense moment while Annie glanced nervously at the three adults, not exactly sure what was going on.

Coach Ritter cleared her throat and took a small step back. "Anyway, I just came by to say you did a great job out there, Annie. I can see you've been putting in extra training. I'm so proud of you."

"Thanks," Annie said.

Dad winked at Coach Ritter and put his arm around Annie's shoulders again. "That's my girl."

"Our girl." Mum folded her arms tightly across her chest. She shifted her weight in her leather boots. "David, I'm absolutely exhausted. Jetlag, you know. Annie, return your skates and let's go. I'm sure you're desperate for a shower."

No, not really. What Annie really wanted to do was have a laugh with the girls in the locker room, chat a bit with Jesse about music, and go to the post-bout party at Lauren's house, where there was a trampoline in the back garden.

Instead, she found herself squashed in Dad's pickup between Mum who was ready to kill Dad, and Dad who had no idea what he had done wrong.

Chapter Twelve

"When I was growing up, we had a tradition of having as many pies as we had people over for Thanksgiving. I've got an apple-peach and a pumpkin cheesecake. What should the third one be?" Dad asked as he rolled out the dough.

The kitchen was filled with dirty pots and utensils, but the smells engulfing it were tantalizing. Roasting turkey and fresh cranberry sauce, spices blending with the sliced fruit. Annie had deliberately eaten only a slice of toast for breakfast, just so she could enjoy the feast. Any minute now her stomach would start moaning.

Annie looked up from the potatoes she was peeling. "Mum likes lemon meringue."

Her parents had barely spoken since the bout last night,

and when they did, it was in stiff, formal tones. No longer were they "Pippa" and "Davy"; the warmth from the first day was long gone.

"Good plan." Dad placed half of the dough in the bottom of the pie pan and dusted it with flour and brown sugar. "I'll put the egg yolks in the cheesecake. Where is your mum anyway?"

Annie sighed. "In her room. Working."

"Ah, of course." A sad smile crossed Dad's face and Annie knew how he felt. Even several thousands of miles away from her office, Mum couldn't stop working, despite being on holiday. But when challenged, she always said that someone had to support the family. Another constant argument between her parents.

"I can ask her to come and help," Annie said.

"Don't bother. It's a small kitchen. And I can do it all. I am the master Thanksgiving chef extraordinaire, muah hahahaha!" Dad puffed out his chest and gave an evil laugh that was cut short by the cranberry sauce boiling over. He quickly rushed over to turn the gas off and gave the sauce a stir. Bringing the wooden spoon to his lips, he blew on it until it was cool enough to taste. He sighed blissfully. "I do love any holiday that involves loads of food."

Annie threw the potatoes in the pot of boiling water, sprinkled in some salt and placed the lid slightly askew to let out the steam. "How come we never celebrated Thanksgiving in London?"

"I kept it up for a while, when you were really little. But it's not a holiday over there. You had school and your mum had work... Things just got complicated." Dad didn't look at her as he went back to weaving the dough strips in a lattice over the apple-peach filling.

"There was that one year, remember? We went to Mum's American colleague's house for Thanksgiving?" Annie began separating the eggs for the meringue, a task she'd always enjoyed since Dad first showed her how to do it.

Dad gave a melodramatic whimper of despair. "Oh, don't remind me. Dry turkey. Mashed potatoes and stuffing from boxes. Cranberry sauce. From a can! Pre-made pumpkin pie mix. I almost needed therapy after that trauma."

"Well this year, the food's going to be gorgeous." Noticing that Dad was distracted as he remembered the disastrous dinner, Annie sneaked a slice of sugar and cinnamon spiced apple from the pie filling. Yum! "Naturally, because I'm helping you."

Dad narrowed his eyes at her and Annie scowled back before the two laughed. They finished the desserts, except for the meringue which had to wait, and got everything else ready before attacking some of the cleaning. An hour later, Dad heaved the turkey out of the oven. It looked so juicy and tender with a few crispy edges around the wings and thighs.

"Go tell your mum dinner is ready," Dad said as he finished whipping the meringue and plopped it on the lemon custard. Finally the oven was clear and the three pies were ready for baking.

Annie stared at the impressive arrangement of food for a second longer. Her mouth watered, that breakfast toast long forgotten. It was all she could do not to tuck in straight away.

With a silent plea to the food to stay put, she rushed to get Mum.

"Mum, Dad said—" Annie stopped short when Mum gave her a disapproving glare.

"Excuse me, Gemma, just one second." Mum covered the phone with her hand. "Annie, I'm working."

"Yeah, but dinner—"

"You and your father can start without me. I'll be there when I'm finished." Mum shooed Annie out of the room and shut the door behind her. Mum hadn't done that since Annie was little and started working longer hours. Annie stared at the closed door for a minute. A few months apart and she had already forgotten all of Mum's work "rules".

Annie found Dad in the living room slouched on the sofa, television on, bare feet on the coffee table, and a beer in his hand. "Let me guess. She'll come when she's done working."

"Yup." Annie collapsed onto the sofa and reached for the raspberry soda Dad had brought for her.

"It's fine." Dad took a sip of his beer. "Gives the flavours more time to soak in and me a chance to catch up with the football. Can't have Thanksgiving without football. Still remember the last time the Chicago Bears won the Super Bowl. 1985 was a great year."

Annie glanced at the game. Green Bay Packers versus the New York Giants. She knew the basic rules of American football from the time Lauren had dragged her to watch Keith play. "Who are you rooting for?"

"Packers. But don't say that to anyone at Rosie Lee's or I might go out of business. Rival team, you know. From Wisconsin."

"Cool." Annie watched for a bit before picking up *The Taming of the Shrew*. Just because she'd seen it performed, didn't mean she wasn't going to finish reading it. Every so often she'd glance up to catch the game. Both teams were playing well and it was nice hanging out with Dad even though she could do that any time. If only Mum didn't have to work so much and would join them. As a family.

Dad suddenly sat up, moving to the edge of the sofa. "Oh, oh, noooo! Did you see that? What a wuss. That linebacker barely touched him and the quarterback fumbled. I think they should strap those boys to some skates and get them to play roller derby in the off-season. You girls could toughen them up."

Annie playfully punched her dad's shoulder.

"Ouch!" He pretended to screech in a high-pitched voice and cowered away from Annie. "Stop!"

Annie hit Dad again before he wrapped an arm around her, pinning her elbows to her side. Annie tried to break free but he held her tight and kissed the top of her head. "Like I said, you can show those boys who's the boss."

"I have to show you who's boss first." Annie squirmed just enough to start tickling Dad. Whether he really was ticklish or just liked pretending, Dad screeched higher than before and threw a cushion at Annie.

As if a cushion could defeat the greatest tickle monster EVER!

"I'm done. We can eat now."

Annie and Dad looked up from attacking each other, both

of them halfway between being on the sofa and on the floor. Mum stood with her arms folded, in her stylish work clothes as if she were actually in her office, rather than thousands of miles away. Annie straightened up and looked down at her faded jeans and sweatshirt. Dad wasn't much better in jogging bottoms and a shirt with holes in the armpits. No wonder Mum wanted to go shopping tomorrow.

"Wouldn't want to keep you waiting," Dad said. If Mum noticed the jibe, she didn't say anything.

Dad carved the turkey and loaded up each plate with a mound of food. Mum stared at her plate for a second then began nibbling around the edges. Annie tasted a bit of everything first, then tried to choose what she wanted to save for last. It was a hard choice considering it was all delicious.

"Everything is fab, Dad." Annie said between mouthfuls.

"Well, of course," Dad said in a mock conceited voice, then returned back to his normal tone. No, not normal. Dad didn't normally focus so hard to make sure the words came out just right. "Is the food OK for you, Philippa?"

Mum didn't look up, just poked at something with her fork. "What is this white stuff in the sweet potatoes?"

"Marshmallows." Dad grinned. "Great idea, right?"

"Not very healthy, is it?" Mum used her fork to pick out the marshmallows and move them to the side of her plate.

Dad stabbed all the marshmallows from his plate, and Mum's, and stuffed the huge white and pink glob into his mouth. "Yum!"

Mum looked disgusted while Dad chewed with his mouth

open. Annie wanted to scold both of them. They weren't even trying to get along. More like they were doing everything *not* to.

"Hey, Mum," Annie said, with too much enthusiasm, "I got a text from Jesse earlier. He just wanted to say again how great it was to meet you and that he hopes you had fun at the bout."

"Fun. Of course." Mum sniffed disapprovingly. "I loved watching my daughter in a tarty outfit get knocked down by other girls in tarty outfits."

Annie blinked a few times as she tried to control her temper. Maybe it would have been better to let Mum be critical and Dad be childish. That way she could have stayed out of the argument.

Too late now.

"What we wear has nothing to do with anything. It definitely doesn't mean we're tarts." Annie spoke as calmly as she could. "In fact, I reveal less in my derby kit than I did in a leotard."

Dad bit back a smile as Annie made her point. But Mum was a top lawyer; she wasn't going to give up on the case without a fight. "But you can get hurt. I don't like you getting shoved around like that. I'm surprised you've only suffered a sprained ankle. Why don't you find a safer sport – tennis, perhaps? Or cross country? You've always enjoyed running."

What? Quit derby? Annie squared her shoulders and sat taller. She had to work hard to keep the fury out of her voice. "I'm NOT giving it up. I got hurt a couple of times in gymnastics and you never talked about me quitting. When Uncle Pete wanted to take up club rugby after uni you encouraged him to give it a go. What's the difference? They're both contact sports."

Mum wasn't going to back down. "Except that Peter is my brother and weighs a hundred kilos. You're my daughter, and a girl. It's a huge difference."

"You always said that girls could do anything that boys could." Annie set down her fork and crossed her arms.

"Strike two," Dad mumbled.

Mum's lips pressed together tightly. "Fine. You're right. I just don't see where this is going to take you in life. It's hardly something you can put on your CV."

"Sure it is," Dad interrupted, although Annie didn't know if it was to help her out, or defeat Mum. "She's being a team player, making quick decisions, and, as you just witnessed, learning to stand up and defend herself. If you look past the booty shorts and fishnets, you'd see she's made great friends on the team. All of whom are smart, strong, and independent young ladies." Dad sat back in the chair looking smug. For good reason: those were exactly the traits Mum valued.

And yet instead of dropping all charges, Mum smirked. "Of course you'd say that. I'm not an idiot, you know."

"What does that mean?" Dad demanded.

Warning bells went off in Annie's head. "Dad, how are those desserts doing? Should we check on them?"

He didn't even glance at the oven, just kept his eyes on Mum.

Now it was Mum's turn to cross her arms. "I know you're having an affair with that coach. I saw you two flirting while Annie and I were getting her skates. You were practically undressing her with your eyes after the match."

"Mum!" Annie choked on her stuffing.

Dad blushed, something he rarely did. "Not true, but my personal life is none of your business. *You* wanted to split up. Besides, Annie can use a strong female role model in her life."

"Dad!" The insult hit Annie as hard as it hit Mum. Annie had rarely seen Mum so livid as she stood up from the table.

Mum's nose flared as she pressed her lips together. "Oh, great role model. A tattooed tart! Annie doesn't need a woman like that. She has me."

Dad stood as well. "Except you're thousands of miles away. *Working.*"

Annie covered her ears. "Stop it! Both of you. You're ruining everything!"

"Fine, I'll go then." Mum threw her napkin on her half-finished meal and stormed into her room. Dad slumped back in his chair and began shovelling food into his mouth as if he hadn't eaten in years. Annie just stared at her plate, tears rolling down her cheeks. A few minutes later, the guest room door opened.

Good, Mum had calmed down. Maybe now they could all make an effort to be a family, even if it was just for Thanksgiving.

Except that Mum had her bags with her. All of them.

"I'm leaving. Annie, if you wish to see me before I fly back home, I'll be staying at the Royal Suites on Maple Avenue."

And with that, she stormed out of the house, slamming the front door behind her.

"No, Mum, wait." Annie got up and rushed outside after her, but the taxi was already driving away.

Chapter Thirteen

"Mum's not answering my calls," Annie told Tyler that evening. She had been desperate to get out of the house and had invited herself over to Tyler's. His family were back from their dinner at the restaurant, his grandparents and uncle were gone, and both his parents were in their respective studies. Annie had brought a huge container of leftover turkey and all of the lemon meringue pie with her to Tyler's. Mum had left before the pie came out of the oven and neither Annie nor Dad wanted it in the house. The tension at home was too much without the pie mocking them.

"She did send me an email, though." Annie spread mayonnaise on a slice of white bread before adding turkey and a bit of lettuce while Tyler helped himself to a huge piece of pie. "Just to say that she needed some space and she'll contact me soon."

"Well, what's the problem? She'll be in touch. Nothing to worry about," Tyler said before spooning a massive bite into his mouth.

Annie closed her sandwich, pressing it down a bit to keep the turkey from falling out. "Yeah, but she's only here for a few days. I don't want to remember her visit this way."

Tyler shrugged. "Then don't think about it."

Annie frowned. Why couldn't Tyler understand? She couldn't just forget about something so important. "I can't help thinking about it. I feel like it's partially my fault. My parents started it, true, but I mentioned roller derby and then it all went crazy. I shouldn't have bothered taking Mum to the bout when I knew she wouldn't like it. Now she wants me to quit."

"She has a point," Tyler said with his mouth full. "It's dangerous and kind of butch, which you're not. Without roller derby, we'd have more time to hang out together."

Meaning she'd have more time to do the things *he* wanted. That didn't seem fair. "You're not being very supportive. Roller derby is my thing. It's what I want to do."

"Why? What do you like so much about it?" Annie knew he was asking it as a rhetorical question, but she decided to answer his question seriously. It was hard to put her feelings into words but she had to make him see, make him understand.

"It's thrilling and unpredictable. One second someone's blocking you, the next you're speeding around the rink. From the first day I watched the Illinoisies play the Corn Hustlers,

I was hooked. And best of all, most of the girls who play are really great."

Annie's face relaxed as she felt the tension lift from her shoulders. This was what she needed to tell Mum. This was how she could get Mum to understand how important it was to her.

Tyler scraped the last of his pie off the plate. "They're great at being freaks."

The smile that had crossed Annie's face as she talked about the sport she loved vanished. "At least they're not full of themselves like your friends. Roller girls are individuals, not afraid to be different. That's what's so great about roller derby. Everyone is welcome."

Tyler rolled his eyes. "That's the only way they'll get enough people to play. It's no big deal making a team that anyone can join."

That wasn't quite true. You had to have the basic skills so you wouldn't get hurt. Annie still remembered the effort she put into making the league, and the sad looks on the faces of the girls who hadn't made the cut.

"What is it with you and roller derby?" Annie set down her half-eaten sandwich. "You're always putting it down. You've only been to that one bout on Halloween. I thought you'd be there yesterday. To cheer me on. I could have done with you being there with my parents at each other's throats."

Tyler set his plate in the sink. "Look, I'm sorry your parents are fighting, but I was busy. Besides, roller derby just isn't my thing."

"Why?"

He didn't even pretend to be ashamed of what he said next. "Well, for one thing, it's embarrassing standing next to you in those freakish clothes and you being so much taller than me in skates."

Annie stood up straight with her shoulders back. "I am taller than you."

"Yeah, and that's just wrong."

"Says who?"

Tyler folded his arms, not looking at her. "It doesn't matter. I just don't like roller derby, OK? There's no point in it and I shouldn't have to pretend."

Annie put her hands on her hips. "Oh right, but you still expect me to go to your soccer games."

"That's different. The whole world plays soccer. You love soccer too."

Love was a very strong word. True she had enjoyed going to a couple of games with Dad in London but it wouldn't bother her if she never saw a match again. "Not really. It's fine, but I only go to the school games for you. And you don't do the same for me. We do everything you want to do. We hang out with your friends, not mine."

Tyler sat on one of the kitchen chairs and leaned the chair back onto two legs. His hands wrapped behind his head. "Yeah, because my friends are actually cool."

"Right – they're so cool, they can't be bothered to make the new girl feel welcome. Even now, I bet half the team don't know my name," Annie said.

Tyler rolled his eyes. "Of course they do. You're popular. You're my girlfriend."

There it was. The truth. She was just the girlfriend of a popular guy. "Exactly. I'm not 'Annie', just 'Tyler's girlfriend'. Your lot never even talk to me."

"Yeah, right. I had to tell Javier to lay off hitting on you."

"Javier is——" Annie stopped. If Tyler didn't know his teammate was gay, it wasn't her place to out him. "He's the only one who's made any effort to include me, even though I've tried to chat with the others. You don't bother to do that with my friends. You've never even tried to be nice to Lexie."

The front legs of Tyler's chair slammed back on the floor. "Oh, please. The other day I swear she was wearing some Amish dress. You should be glad you don't have to hang out with that freak show any more."

Annie could feel her nose flaring as her lips pressed tight. "She's not a freak show. And neither are my teammates. Lexie is the most talented person I know. She doesn't have to pretend to be someone she's not just to fit in. And I never *had* to hang out with her. I wanted to."

"Right. Which is why you guys are always together." His comment hurt more than she wanted to admit. He was right. She didn't hang out with Lexie any more. Because of him.

"You made me feel guilty for not spending time with you. It's always you, you, you. Not any more. You keep your friends, I'll keep mine."

Tyler stood up with his arms crossed across his chest. "Do you know how lucky you are? Half the girls at school would kill to be seen with me. They don't get why I'm with a roller girl."

"More like why a roller girl is bothering with you." She grabbed her coat and let her voice echo throughout the whole house. "Form an orderly queue here, girls! He's all yours."

She picked up the remaining three quarters of the lemon meringue pie and was just about to fling it in his face when Tyler's mother walked into the kitchen. Instead, Annie stuffed the pie in the bin. He hadn't even thanked her for bringing it. Or complimented it. Ungrateful pig.

Without looking at either Tyler or Mrs Erickson, Annie pulled her hat down hard around her ears before flinging the front door wide open.

"Annie, wait. That's not what I meant. Come back!"

But Annie ignored him as she stomped home along the cold dark streets. Stupid, chauvinistic, hypocritical, condescending, arrogant idiot! He basically called *her* a freak. How could he? Oh, how she hated him right now.

Since she'd first set eyes on him, all Annie wanted was to date Tyler, the boy who made her swoon just at the thought of him. Now she had him but what did that mean? He was an unsupportive freak-hater. Not cool. So not cool.

She tried to bundle her coat more tightly around her but the chill went through to her bones. She looked behind her. Nothing. There was no one there. He could have at least come after her. Driven up and offered to take her home in his car. Did this mean they were over? Was she really going to get to school on Monday and find a queue of giggling girls waiting to be his next prize? Oh, crumbs. What had she done? She looked over her shoulder again.

Maybe I should go back and apologize.

No. She continued towards home. He needed to apologize to her. For putting down the people and things she loved. For expecting her to share his interests, but not caring about hers. For wanting her to be someone she wasn't. And most of all for dissing Lexie.

Annie pulled her phone out of her pocket and scrolled down to Lexie's number. But instead of calling her, Annie shoved the phone back in her jeans. Lexie wouldn't understand. If anything, she'd be happy Annie got what she deserved.

"I don't need a boy to make me happy," Lexie had said that day in the cafeteria. Annie had a boy, the best looking boy she'd ever met. But now she was walking home alone in the cold.

Some happiness.

Some Thanksgiving.

The dry leaves tumbled across the pavement as Annie stopped suddenly. A deep chill ran through her body that had nothing to do with the wind. Oh dear. She could see what she had done now.

She'd stormed out – just like her mum.

Chapter Fourteen

Tyler: hey babe sorry about the other day. forgive me?

Annie: Maybe. Will you come to my next bout? It's the championship one.

Tyler: wouldnt miss it

Annie held the phone against her chest after rereading the texts she and Tyler had sent each other. They'd made up. Good. That's what she wanted, of course. Except now, when she thought of him, she didn't have that tingling sensation running through her body. *What a shame*, she thought as she slipped the phone back in her pocket. She supposed that giddy feeling couldn't last forever. At least they were still together and would hang out tomorrow. But today it was Mum Day. Annie couldn't believe her mother's visit was already almost over and that she was flying back to London tonight.

They had both apologized and patched things up but Annie still felt a bit awkward as she watched her mum packing up her things at the hotel. If only Mum didn't live so far away.

"When will I see you again?" Annie asked.

"Whenever you like, sweetheart." Mum stopped folding a pair of trousers to stare at Annie. "Seriously. You say the word and your ticket is booked. Even if it's just for a long weekend. Deal?"

"Yes, thanks." Annie shifted from one foot to the other. "You know I miss you a lot when you're not here, don't you?"

Mum stopped packing to walk around the bed and give Annie a hug. "And I miss you. Everything in the flat reminds me of you. It's hard sometimes."

They held each other until Annie pulled away. She could have stayed like that forever, but Mum would be upset if she missed her flight.

"How are you doing for time?" Annie asked.

Mum didn't even look at the clock on the bedside table. "I'm fine. Here, look through this pile of clothes." Mum set a large plastic carrier bag on the bed. "I brought a few bits and pieces from London. No pressure. Whatever doesn't fit or you don't like, I'll return."

"Ta." Annie looked through the things. They had gone shopping at the mall yesterday, especially for bras and pyjamas, but these were things Mum had brought with her from London.

On top were socks and underwear. Of course Mum would remember the essentials. Good thing. Annie could do with some new underwear and the knickers Mum picked out were cute boy shorts. There were also a few jumpers, three tops, a swishy skirt, skinny jeans, a few pairs of tights, and wool-lined slippers. They all fitted and Annie loved everything. Mum had always had great taste in clothes. "I'll take the lot, if that's OK."

"Perfect, I'm glad you like them." Mum smiled. "Even with you so far away, I like picking things out for you. Makes me feel like I'm still a part of your life."

Annie looked at her trainers. It wasn't fair. She shouldn't have spent half the visit fighting with Mum. "I'm sorry."

"I know. And I am too. I would have stayed longer, but because it's not a holiday at home I have to get back to work."

Annie wanted to ask if Mum would take the train straight to the office when she got in, even though it would be a Sunday, but she didn't. The last thing she wanted was another argument. "Will you get some sleep on the plane?"

"Unlikely, but that's just how things go." Mum zipped up her bag. She squinted at the clock and turned to Annie. "Well that's me sorted. The airport van won't pick me up for another hour and a half. How about a run? It's nice and sunny outside and I fancy a bit of exercise before being cooped up in the plane."

A workout session with Mum? Why not – Annie was already wearing trainers and a tracksuit. "Yeah, that would be brilliant!"

Mum unzipped her suitcase and pulled out some workout clothes and trainers. Annie wouldn't be surprised if Mum had picked the hotel just for its twenty-four-hour gym to fit around her itinerary. Mum was ready in a couple of minutes and when they left, her phone stayed on the bedside table.

"Where are we going?" Mum asked as they started jogging. Annie looked around quickly to get herself orientated. The hotel was near the business park, between Rosie Lee's in the downtown and the roller rink on the outskirts.

"There's a nice park not too far away. We can run around it and head back?"

"Will it take less than an hour?"

"Fifty minutes tops."

"Let's do it."

Mum set the pace which Annie easily matched. She couldn't remember the last time they had run together. Usually Mum went to the gym where she could work and run at the same time.

"It's great being outside instead of multitasking on a treadmill." Mum must have read Annie's mind. "Trust me, it's not easy to send emails while you're on a machine."

Annie reached out and gave her mum's hand a squeeze. "This was a great idea. I've been feeling a bit sluggish with all the food I've eaten over the past few days."

Mum let out a sigh; it was a couple of minutes before she spoke again. "I want to apologize again for Thanksgiving."

"It's OK—" Annie started but Mum cut her off.

"No, it's not OK. I acted poorly. I guess I was feeling left out. You and your father obviously have your own lives here and seem to be doing fine without me. I felt like you didn't need me any more."

"Of course we need you. Or I do at least." Annie glanced at Mum as they kept running. Mum had always been the strong, independent one. Annie never imagined her as vulnerable, but that was how she was coming across now.

Mum shook her head as if trying to rid herself of those weak emotions, only to replace them with bitter ones. "Only until your father gets together with that Ritter woman."

Annie pressed her lips together. Dad didn't talk about Coach Ritter to her, but she had definitely noticed sparks between them for a while. She didn't really want to think of anyone else with Dad besides Mum, but he could do much worse than Coach Ritter. Even if she had benched Annie.

"There's only one Mum, and that's you."

"Thanks, sweetheart. It's just hard for me to accept he's moving on. One of my girlfriends is trying to convince me to put a dating profile up online, but I can't. I really can't. I'm not there yet." Mum shook her head, sending her short ponytail swinging. "Your dad and I have only just agreed to formally file for divorce while I've been here."

Annie grabbed Mum's hand again and this time didn't let go straight away. "When did you stop loving Dad?"

"Oh, Annie. That's complicated. The short answer is that we're too different to make things work any more."

They looked both ways before crossing a busy street and then they were at the park.

"But weren't you always different?" Annie asked.

"Yes, but I guess it didn't matter so much at first. Or we chose not to let it matter."

"Tell me again how you two met." Annie knew the story, but it had been a long time since she'd heard Mum's version of it.

Mum was panting a bit now but a small smile crossed her face as she reminisced.

"You know Davy was at uni in London, right? He came over to study for a year. One night, I went to a friend's party, and there was this long-haired man playing his guitar softly in the corner."

Annie grinned. "I still can't believe you fell for a headbanger."

Mum smiled back, although her smile was a bit sadder. "Trust me, he wasn't my type, and it was years before he agreed to cut his hair. That night, I went into the room where he was playing and he started singing that he'd like to cook me dinner. I told him to sod off, assuming he was sloshed, which he was, and that he'd forget about me in the morning. But he didn't. The next day, he rang and asked if I liked *duck à l'Orange* – in a horrid French accent I might add. I couldn't say no. It was the best meal I'd ever eaten and by the end of the evening I was completely smitten. Won over by music and food. I'm such a cliché, eh?"

It was pretty much the story Annie knew, but when Dad told it, he'd say he'd fallen in love with the beautiful, long-haired English girl at first sight, and he'd always break into a cringey rendition of the song he sang that night. "And now you hate him."

Mum stopped running and pushed her glasses up her nose to stare at Annie. "Sweetheart, I could never hate your father. He was the best husband and friend. But eventually music and food wasn't enough. We changed and we're better apart now. Surely you must see that."

"I guess. But it makes me feel split up too that I can't be with both of you."

Mum started jogging again. "I know. When I said I wanted a separation, it didn't even occur to me that he would move back here, and take you with him. I sometimes wonder if I would have suggested it if I had known what would happen."

Annie didn't challenge that. She knew Mum loved her, but she also finally admitted to herself that their divorce was for the best. It was just hard to let go of the past.

"I'm afraid Tyler and I are going to break up. We had a row the other day. We're cool now, but he said some things that hurt." Annie kept her eyes on the path but could feel Mum's stare.

"He's not pressuring you to do more than you're ready for, is he?"

Annie shook her head. "Not like that, but he doesn't like me playing roller derby. He thinks it takes up too much of my time. He says it's unfeminine and that girls who play are freaks."

Mum's stare shifted between Annie, the running path, and back at Annie. It took her a few moments to reply. "You know I'm not a fan of the whole roller derby scene. I'm afraid you're going to get hurt. But I can see how good it's been for you. It's made you more assertive, and I know how much you love it. I wouldn't take away something that means that much to you."

Annie released the tension she hadn't realized she had been holding in since Thanksgiving. "Good, because I would have put up a big fight."

Mum chuckled, then grew serious again. "What bothers me is Tyler's attitude. It's not his place to tell you what to do, especially when it's something you enjoy and do so well."

"You think I'm good?"

"Of course. When you like something, you've always given it your all. You're my daughter, after all."

"Thanks. And you're right," Annie said. "I'm not quitting, and Tyler did say he'd go to my next bout."

"Good. That sounds a bit more like it."

They turned a corner and Annie caught sight of a familiar shape huddled on a park bench with a sketchbook perched against her knees.

"Hey!" Annie called out, heading over to the bench. "You're back from Indiana."

Lexie's head jerked up. She slammed the book shut and ran off in the other direction. Pretty fast for someone who always said she wasn't athletic. Within seconds, Lexie had disappeared.

Annie slowed down and stopped in front of the bench where Lexie had been sitting. Three coloured pencils lay on the ground under the bench. Annie picked them up and held them in her hand. One of them, the brown one, had snapped in half.

"Who was that?" Mum asked.

"Lexie."

"Your best friend? Is she shy?"

Annie shook her head. Lexie was anything but shy. "We, uh, had a bit of a falling out."

"Oh?"

"She and Tyler don't get on." Annie wasn't sure how much she wanted to tell Mum, but it slipped out anyway. "And I may have chosen to hang out with him a bit more than her."

Mum shook her head. Her disappointment was clear. "You know, Annie, romance is great, but real friendships last forever. It hasn't been easy over the last few months with you being gone. I don't know where I'd be without my friends' support."

Annie glanced at Mum, feeling like she was discovering parts of her she had never known. Could the constant criticism be Mum's way of hiding her vulnerability?

"I'm sorry, Mum. I didn't know."

Mum glanced at her watch and they picked up the pace. "Of course you didn't. I didn't want you to. And I certainly don't want you to worry about me now. Like I said, I have my friends."

"I've been trying to talk to Lexie, but you see what happens when I try," Annie grumbled, clutching the coloured pencils as her feet pounded the path.

"Sometimes talking isn't enough."

"I really miss her."

"I'm sure she misses you too. Why don't you try *showing* her how you feel?"

They left the park and started heading back to the hotel. Mum took a deep breath and seemed to hesitate before asking, "Sweetheart, do any of your friends like Tyler?"

Annie remembered Lauren's scolding look when Annie missed practice to help Tyler study. Lauren obviously wasn't a fan. But most of the other girls on the team agreed he was hot. That meant they liked him, right? *Liked to look at him*, Annie argued with herself. That wasn't the same as liking – or disliking – him as a person. And if they knew he called them freaks… No, they wouldn't be friends.

"My friends don't hang out in the same crowd as him, so they don't really know him."

But Annie had said enough for Mum to draw her own conclusions.

"There are always going to be some people who don't like each other, that's normal. But if *none* of your friends get along with Tyler, maybe you should wonder why."

Annie wanted to tell her mum that she was wrong, that Annie's friends and Tyler were different. That was it. Roller girls didn't really mix with jocks and cheerleaders. *But it wasn't just her friends*, another voice in her head argued. Other than Javier, none of Tyler's friends seemed to like her. No, more like they didn't notice her. None of that felt right.

They got back to the hotel with just enough time for Mum to shower and change back into her business suit. Just as Mum finished paying her bill, the van arrived to take her to the airport.

Annie set down the carrier bag of new clothes and flung her arms around Mum in a tight hug. Oh, she was really going to miss her. Dad was good fun to be around and was her number one fan, but he wasn't much good for girl talk.

They held each other until the driver cleared his throat. Mum turned away quickly, but Annie still caught the tears behind her glasses.

"Call me when you land," Annie said, not caring that she sounded like the mum instead of the daughter.

"It'll be two o'clock in the morning."

"I don't care. I just want to know you're OK."

Mum nodded, brushing away her tears. "Of course. And I meant what I said – whenever you want to come back, just let me know. Hopefully it'll be for good once this year's up, but that's your choice. I love you."

"Love you too, Mum." Annie waved as Mum got into the van. She didn't care if Mum saw the tears rolling down her cheeks.

She'd always thought she made the right choice in living with Dad. Now, watching Mum wave from the van window as it drove away, she wasn't so sure any more.

Chapter Fifteen

Annie dragged her feet into the roller rink for practice on Monday. She missed Mum more than she had when she and Dad had first moved away, and wanted nothing more than to stay at home with a bowl of Dad's caramel popcorn and watch *Mamma Mia* on DVD.

Keep busy, Mum would say. *When things are looking down, keep busy and you'll soon start to feel better.*

Besides, even though Annie thought she had a good reason to miss practice, she wasn't going to do that to her team again. Not when there was the possibility of Coach benching her for the championship bout.

"Annie," Sharmila called, looking up from the phone everyone was crowded around. "Did I tell you? My whole family loved your mum. One auntie made me promise to get her number so they can have her over for tea."

Annie gave her a small smile. "She'd love that. Cheers."

"Come see the wedding photos," Sharmila said, pointing to her phone.

Annie looked over Sharmila's shoulder at some of the photos. All the women were in colourful saris. Sharmila's sister, Priya, looked radiant in her elaborate purple sari, wedding jewellery and make-up – but no nose ring, Annie noticed. There were also photos of the ceremony at a temple and then the reception at a hall.

"Dang, you're *smoking* in that sari," Holly said, prodding Sharmila's shoulder. "Think you can get me one?"

Annie turned away. Not to be rude, but the pictures of Sharmila's happy family just made her miss Mum and reminded her of how their family used to be.

"Hey, why so down?" Jesse came up and placed a hand on Annie's shoulder.

"Mum's gone back to the UK. And part of me wishes I was with her."

"For real?" Jesse's eyes widened under his shaggy hair.

Annie sniffed and felt a lump build in the back of her throat. "I don't know. I miss her a lot."

"Come 'ere." Jesse held his arms open wide and Annie fell into them. She couldn't remember hugging him before and it felt nice to have his support. Under his long-sleeved T-shirt advertising a brand of skateboards, his arms felt surprisingly strong. "Well, I'd miss you if you left. Really."

Annie rested her head on his shoulder for a second before pulling away. "Thanks. I'd miss you too."

He grinned and she knew she hadn't been just saying it to be polite. She really would miss Jesse, and all her roller derby mates, massively.

She got her gear on and joined rest of the team on the rink, although Sharmila was still taking about the wedding throughout their warm-ups.

"All right, peeps." Coach Ritter clapped her hands. "I know you all have lots to talk about, but we need to get cracking. Next bout is our championship one and we're most likely competing against the High Rollers."

Everyone groaned. The High Rollers had been league champions for several years and they were the Liberty Belles' arch rivals. Annie felt her left ankle, which hadn't hurt in over a month, twinge. She'd sprained it when Dee Stroyer, a High Roller, had played dirty.

"Don't let them intimidate you," Coach Ritter continued. "Remember, you're better than they are. In all regards. Everyone played great at the last bout and if we keep that up, we have a good shot at becoming league champions."

The girls cheered. In the background, Annie heard Jesse cheering too. He was the league's MC, and was sometimes called in to ref as well; he shouldn't play favourites. But it cheered Annie up a bit to know he was on their side.

"So let's keep up the hard work with some Gruesome

Twosomes."

"I call Carmen," Holly said and she and Carmen immediately linked arms.

Some others paired up too. Lauren picked up Annie's hand and Annie gave it a friendly squeeze. She hadn't played this game before, but Lauren had never let her down.

Coach Ritter looked around at the pairs and changed a few people around. "In this game I'd like you to be with a girl who has opposite skills to you so you can learn to work together. If you're quick, then I want you with someone who's slower."

Annie and Lauren leaned into each other and grinned. They were probably the two biggest extremes on the team both in appearance and skills. Lauren was about seven inches shorter and ten kilos heavier than Annie. While they were both great skaters, Annie had the speed while Lauren had the stability. Together, they'd be unstoppable!

"Liz and Sharmila will start being IT. If they tag you, count to five and then you're IT. The pair that gets tagged the least times will be our winners. Here's the catch. You and your partner have to be in contact all the time, whether you're tagging or being tagged. If you are not touching for more than a second, you're out. Jesse, you want to help keep score and monitor the pairs?" Coach Ritter asked.

Annie grinned as Jesse nodded eagerly as he put on some skates. Although he was more into skateboarding, he was just as good on roller skates. If the roller derby league were co-ed, Annie was sure Jesse would be on the team. Would Tyler even consider playing roller derby?

Coach Ritter blew her whistle and Annie pushed that thought out of her mind. No point in wondering, as the league only allowed girls. Besides, she and Lauren had Liz and Sharmila to avoid. They dodged them easily but a minute later Tashi and Natalia were IT and Natalia's hand reached out to touch Annie's shoulder. Now Annie and Lauren were IT!

Hands clasped together, Annie and Lauren dashed towards Carmen and Holly skating together on the other side of the rink. Annie's hand almost slipped out of Lauren's but Lauren held her tight. Annie reached out with the other hand and caught Holly just as the short girl was trying to twist out of the way.

Annie and Lauren knew Carmen and Holly were going to try to tag them right back. Annie and Lauren skated away as fast as possible with the other two girls hot on their tails. Annie was sure they were going to catch them when instinctively she and Lauren switched to backward skating, changed hands, and watched Carmen lose her balance and land laughing on her kneepads.

Annie and Lauren passed Jesse and he gave them a discreet thumbs up.

By the end of the game, Annie and Lauren were the only pair caught just once; everyone else had been tagged lots of times. It didn't matter that they were an odd couple. Together they made the perfect team.

"Great work, everyone," Coach Ritter said. "Now let's try out some strategies for the championship bout."

It was a gruelling session and by the time they finished

everyone was completely wiped out. Annie couldn't speak for the others, but she at least felt ready to take on the High Rollers – and win.

If she could move by then, that is. Just taking off her pads felt like an effort. The others seemed to think so too. Liz was guzzling water and Lauren was sprawled out on the floor. Still, it was a good feeling. Being tired and sweaty from roller derby was always a good thing.

"On the first day of derby, my tough coach said to me…" Carmen started to sing to the tune of "The Twelve Days of Christmas". She paused for a moment and Lauren improvised instead.

"You're the girl in a helmet panty!"

Everyone, including Jesse and Coach Ritter, laughed. By the time all the skates and pads were off, they had rewritten the whole carol. It wasn't musically perfect, but still they made it work to the tune.

"Twelve fans a-cheering, eleven seconds ticking, ten skaters skating, nine bruises aching, eight wheels a-rolling, seven holes in bright tights, six players swearing, fiiiiive points ahead! Four blockers down, three referees, two jammers score, and a girl in a helmet pann-teee!"

Everyone cheered and started hugging each other. Ever the show-off, Holly stood on a threadbare bench and started blowing kisses at everyone. Right now, surrounded by her roller derby friends, Annie felt like she could take on the world. No matter what happened at the championship bout, she knew her friends would still be together, regardless of the final score. And that was more important than winning or losing. A good friendship should last for a long time.

Not just a couple of months.

With a pang, Annie thought of Lexie.

She had been ignoring the situation for a while. She knew she hadn't been a good friend to Lexie. She was going to change. Effective immediately.

Chapter Sixteen

Annie had inherited her dad's sense of humour and her mum's determination, but neither of her parents had passed on any artistic genes. She had spent half the night preparing cupcakes for Lexie and they still weren't as detailed as Lexie could have made them with her eyes closed. Even if they weren't perfect, Annie hoped the message was clear and that in the end, it would be the thought that counted. And the taste. That part at least had turned out perfectly.

Now to find Lexie before classes started.

And corner her so she wouldn't run off again.

Annie found her friend by her locker. Lexie's hair was back to its wild ringlets. In terms of fashion, today Lexie almost looked like everyone else at school with skinny jeans and a jacket.

But on closer inspection, Annie could see that the jacket had been a patchwork quilt in a previous life. And yet Lexie made it look fabulous.

"Lexie, I'm really, really sorry I've been a self-absorbed idiot." Annie spoke quickly, afraid that Lexie would run off. Lexie shifted her weight but didn't move from her place. Nor did she look at Annie. Annie took a deep breath and kept on. "I should never have let anyone get between us, no matter how gorgeous they might be. I was daft and I'm really sorry. I promise it'll never happen again. I've brought a peace offering."

Annie held out the container she had lined with Grandma's lace napkins – Dad had made it clear he didn't mind if the napkins never found their way back to the house. The two coloured pencils she had picked up under the park bench were perched on either side of the cupcakes as if standing guard.

Lexie looked into the plastic container and her eyes widened. She glanced at Annie for the briefest second and then looked back at the cupcakes. Annie saw that as a hint to continue.

"I used the Earl Grey with lavender icing recipe we invented together and then added food colouring as a tribute to your favourite artists. This one," she pointed to the cake with a banana on top, "is the Warhol one, obviously. It was a real pain to make. But I thought a banana would be easier to do than a Campbell's soup tin."

Lexie made a sound that sounded almost like a chuckle. Annie's spirits lifted just a bit as she pointed to the abstract one with graphic squares.

"This one here is supposed to be Mondrian. I know the lines aren't perfectly straight but it turned out better than I expected. And this is—" Annie pointed to the cupcake that said, *"Ceci est un cupcake."*

"Magritte," Lexie interrupted with amused eyes. "But isn't it supposed to say, *'Ceci n'est pas'*?"

Now it was Annie's turn to be amused. She knew French fairly well, but had looked up the artist's logic last night. "His painting of a pipe says, 'This is not a pipe,' because it wasn't really a pipe. It was just a painting of one. But this really IS a cupcake, so I wasn't going to say it wasn't."

Lexie nodded. "Obviously. And this last one?"

Annie grinned at the cupcake which had erupted over the sides. It was definitely her favourite and had been the easiest to make since it had happened accidentally. Still, she felt quite clever for seeing the potential in the mistake. "That's the Dalí one."

Lexie's face twitched as if she was trying hard not to give in and break into a smile.

Annie placed the cupcake container in Lexie's hands. "I know I've been a horrible friend and I'm sorry. Will you give me another chance?"

Lexie set the container in her locker, but not before she broke off a piece of the Dalí cupcake and savoured it. "I suppose."

Annie squealed and flung her arms around Lexie. "I'm so glad. This afternoon, what are you doing? Are you free? What would you like to do?"

"Thrift store browsing?"

"Perfect!"

Lexie took the remaining Dalí cupcake out before sealing the container and shutting her locker. "These are amazing. Cheers m'dear."

Annie linked her arm through Lexie's and cheered herself inside. Lexie was using British expressions she'd picked up from Annie again. They were good. Life was good. Everything was good. School was great.

Well, maybe that was going too far.

Annie and Lexie went separate ways when they got to Annie's English class. The first sight that met Annie's eyes was Kelsey and Tyler talking. To make it even worse, Kelsey was perched on top of Tyler's desk.

Just because Kelsey's putting on moves doesn't mean Tyler's interested, Annie tried to convince herself. OK, she and Tyler were cool now, maybe even better than before. Still, his comment about girls dying to go out with him still left a wound. Probably because she knew it was true.

"Hi, guys," Annie said, trying to sound as cool and nonchalant as she could. Tyler got up and came over to give her a kiss. It was a good one, no doubt, but it didn't leave her weak at the knees like his kisses used to. Maybe it was better that way. She liked having more control of the relationship.

"Hey, want to hang out after soccer practice?" Tyler asked. "Some of the guys were asking about you."

Annie knew that was a bit far-fetched, unless by "some of the

148

guys" Tyler meant Javier, but it was still nice of him to try and make her feel included. "Sorry. Lexie and I are going shopping."

"Hope she's not taking you to get a jacket like the one she's wearing today," Tyler teased. "I think she stole it from my grandmother's sofa." It was meant as a joke, she knew that, but it stung as a snide remark towards her best friend.

"Actually, she got it from my grandmother's sofa," Annie teased back, but gave him a look that warned him not to comment further. It worked on Tyler, not on Kelsey.

"Oh, god. That girl dresses like such a freak." Kelsey scrunched up her nose in disgust.

Even though the dreaded "f" word made Annie flinch inside, she still smiled sweetly at Kelsey. "You're welcome to join us. We might find something for you to wear that isn't totally boring and lacking in personality."

Tyler's mouth twitched and a couple of other kids giggled while Kelsey gave Annie the finger. Mission: "Fire Clever Comeback at Kelsey" accomplished!

Ms Schwartz called the class to settle down. "All right. You should have all finished reading *The Taming of the Shrew*. If you didn't, and you watched the movie or read a summary online, trust me, I'll know. So, what did we think? Is it cruel and misogynistic? A love story? A satire? Anyone who speaks up gets extra credit."

Three hands immediately shot up in the air. Annie's was one of them. The C+ from that last essay was still painful and she wanted to improve her overall grade.

Ms Schwartz rubbed her palms as she looked around. Finally she nodded at Annie.

"It's partly a love story," Annie said. "But mostly it's about knowing how to play the game. Petruchio's pride is damaged by Katherine getting the better of him. He can't accept that a woman is his equal."

Ms Schwartz mulled over Annie's words for a few seconds before nodding her head in agreement. "Very good point. Who else? Elijah?"

"Surprise, surprise. A feminist roller girl," Kelsey hissed while Elijah offered his take on the play. "When's the next bra-burning?"

Annie didn't say anything. Not because she couldn't think of a good comeback – she could think of several – but because Kelsey was right. And Annie didn't mind in the least. Roller girls were feminists, and so was she.

Like Mum.

Like Lexie.

Annie was in good company.

Annie and Lexie met outside school and headed straight downtown. There was only one cupcake left in the container, the Warhol one, and Lexie offered it to Annie, who declined. Annie had all her botched attempts at icing a banana at home and it was never polite to eat the gifts you'd given.

Downtown Liberty Heights was streaming with people making a start on their Christmas shopping. Not only that, it looked like the city had invested in every single Christmas decoration known to man, elf, and reindeer. And Annie had thought the Thanksgiving decorations were impressive! Lights adorned everything. If it didn't have lights, it had garlands, wreaths, and ribbons. A window artist had painted festive scenes on different shops. Snowflakes made from paper, plastic, or foam hung from shopfronts. Live animals stood behind a fence for a church's nativity scene. A man in a Father Christmas costume was ringing a bell for donations for the homeless shelter.

Annie couldn't believe Christmas was just around the corner. In a few weeks she and Dad, as well as Aunt Julie and her family in Seattle, would all fly down to Florida and spend Christmas with her grandparents. Time seemed to go by so fast lately.

They went into the second-hand shop and came out with lederhosen, a multi-coloured hat shaped like a glove, fifteen-centimetre platform heels, and sparkly silver leggings. The leggings were for Annie; they'd be perfect for roller derby.

At the jewellery shop, Annie found some stunning earrings made by a local artist. They were turquoise and amber and the proceeds went to a charity supporting women's education in developing countries. Perfect for Mum.

"I'm really bummed I didn't get to meet her," Lexie said after Annie filled her in on what had happened during the visit. "That day in the park, I'm sorry I ran off. I should have just told you I was feeling hurt, instead of sulking."

Annie paid for Mum's present before giving Lexie a squeeze. They headed to a gift shop that had a lot of novelty items. "I don't blame you for running off, after the way I treated you. But have you any idea how fast you are? With some training, you could run the hundred metres."

Lexie laughed. "No way, not happening. My legs were killing me afterwards. I'll leave the running to you jocks."

"I don't think Mum would appreciate being called a jock," Annie teased.

Lexie nodded. "I don't blame her. Speaking of jocks, how's the king of jock-dom?"

Annie noticed the sarcastic tone but at least Lexie was making an effort by asking.

"Tyler? He's fine. Just not as fun as you are. Especially when it comes to shopping."

Lexie turned away from the mirror with a pink wig, chunky clip-on earrings, and tiny round sunglasses that barely shielded her pupils. "Really? I wonder why."

Annie put on some reindeer antlers and galloped around Lexie. "Gooooo, Stags!"

Lexie laughed. "And to think you could have been a cheerleader."

The shopkeeper gave them a scolding look that said, "Buy something or get out, and don't you dare think of taking a five-finger discount." Because of the shopkeeper's rudeness, the girls didn't buy anything, although Lexie swore she would return on a different day for the sunglasses.

The sun had set but it was hardly dark with all the festive lights on. "Where to next?" Lexie asked.

"I drew Sharmila in the Secret Santa exchange. I thought of getting her make-up," Annie said.

"I know just the thing. I got it for myself the other day." Lexie led the way to a small accessories store. From the shelf Lexie pulled down a glittery make-up kit in a pretty case.

"All natural products, no animal testing, and comes off easily without any irritation," Lexie said.

"Perfect." Annie hadn't needed any persuasion. As soon as Lexie handed it to her, Annie knew it had Sharmila's name all over it.

Back outside, snowflakes started to fall. Lexie caught some on her tongue while lots more clung to Annie's eyelashes.

"I still owe you a hot chocolate with whipped cream and extra marshmallows. Let's go to Rosie Lee's?" Annie asked.

Lexie sighed as if it were a huge compromise. "If you insist. And I'll take that scone you offered me the other day too."

Annie grinned. Mum had been right: sometimes talking wasn't enough. But baked goods always did the trick. Especially when they came from Rosie Lee's. "That particular scone has already gone to Happy Tummy Land, but I'm sure I can find you a suitable replacement."

Lexie pretended to stomp on the ground and pout, but slipped on the icy pavement. Annie caught her friend's arm before Lexie fell on her bum. With Annie holding her steady, Lexie was able to regain her balance. "Thanks. Now I know why I like roller derby.

There's no bringing you girls down."

Annie pretended to show off her muscles and then laughed. "I've been doing extra training to get ready for our championship bout. Will you come? I've really missed having you cheering us on."

"Me too. I've missed seeing the Liberty Belles kicking butt."

"If I ever act like such an idiot again, you have full permission to kick MY butt – or at least send me to the penalty box."

Annie linked her arm through Lexie's and started singing the Pogues' "Christmas in New York", but changed the lyrics from New York to Liberty Heights. Lexie laughed, then joined in. To the amusement of the other Christmas shoppers, they sang loudly all the way to Rosie Lee's. Mum was so right. Romance was great, but nothing beat a true friendship.

Chapter Seventeen

"We have gingerbread, we have almond shortbread. *Lebkuchen* and *pepparkakor*. Chocolate truffles covered in powdered sugar to look like snowballs. What other Christmassy treat do we need?" Dad called from the kitchen at Rosie Lee's several days later. There were no customers in the café at the moment but it had been busy all day so Dad was happy. As always, slow periods were a chance to tidy up, restock, and bake. There was always something to do these days; it had been a long time since Annie had been bored at Rosie Lee's.

Annie looked up from stuffing the napkin dispensers. "What about eggnog cookies with peppermint cream on top?"

"Ooh! I've never tried those two flavours together."

Annie shook her head. "I was teasing. I think you have plenty."

"Still … maybe I'll try making peppermint whipped cream. That would go great with the hot chocolates. My hot chocolate vill take over ze vorld! Ha ha!" Dad laughed an evil laugh and twiddled his thumbs like a criminal mastermind.

Annie grinned. "If that's the evilest thing you've got, you better try a new profession."

Dad raised an eyebrow as he rubbed the stubble on his chin. "Hmm, we'll see. Speaking of food, did you eat?"

"I had half a sandwich, but I can't eat much more. I'm too nervous about the championship bout." *No, Annie, don't think like that. Focus on how well everyone's been skating.* "At least we can only end up in second place this year, instead of at the bottom like last year. I'm glad I wasn't here to see that. So sad."

Dad raised his nose high in the air. "That's because last year the Liberty Belles didn't have the one and only daughter of David Turner, the handsome, wonderful, dashing, clever, chef extraordinaire."

Silly Dad, but Annie kissed him anyway. So she was an asset to the team, but no more important than any other member. They just had the advantage of working well together this year.

The door jingled open and a pair of antlers appeared at the entrance, swinging from side to side. The antlers lifted up to reveal Lauren, who was wearing them on her helmet. She made an odd sound before bursting into a laugh. "Can you believe I have no idea what noise a reindeer makes? What kind of animal lover am I?"

"Don't reindeer just laugh and call each other names?" Dad

said, leaning against the doorframe separating the kitchen from the rest of the café.

"Except when they shout out with glee. Ooh!" Lauren helped herself to a couple of cookies from the tray Annie offered her. "Are these those Swedish spice cookies? I think we got them once from Ikea."

"Ja, we call them *pepparkakor*, ja," Dad said in a singsong Swedish accent.

Annie rolled her eyes. "Dad, stick to the baking and leave the voices to actors."

Dad knocked his heels together, threw his shoulders back, and raised his hand in a military salute. "Yes, ma'am. Roger that!"

"No more sugar for you, young man," Annie teased as she grabbed her bag. "You're still coming, right?"

Dad switched from a soldier's voice to a wide-eyed country boy in a second. "Oh, is the biggest bout of the century today? Well, shucks, I forgot. Since they won't let parents be NSOs for the championship, there's no point in me going."

Annie stuck her tongue out at her dad. "See you there."

"The pepper-caker thingies are amazing," Lauren said. "I better take one for Keith too."

"That's my kind of girl, always remembering the help." Dad handed her a few more cookies for the road. "Knock those High Rollers up. I mean down!"

Annie and Lauren got to the car where Lauren's brother Keith was waiting for them. He looked impatient until Lauren offered him a *pepparkakor*, which he downed in one bite. Through the

157

rear mirror, he gave Annie a thumbs up. Lauren took off her helmet so the antlers wouldn't get bent on the car's roof. Annie pulled out her own helmet, which Lexie had decorated for her at the start of the season with an Andy Warhol-esque portrait, and showed off the tinsel she had hung around the edges.

"It looks like I'm wearing a silver wig underneath the helmet, but I don't care," Annie said.

Lauren shrugged. "Well, I'm pretending the dog hair on my tights is reindeer hair and I'm getting Sharmila to give me a red nose."

Annie could see Lauren the Red-Nosed Reindeer in her mind. "If anyone can 'guide' the sleigh, it's you!"

They got to the rink and instead of dropping them off by the door like he normally did, Keith parked the car.

"You're watching us, Keith?" Annie asked.

"Are you kidding? Football season's over and I love seeing my little sister get beaten up. It gives me a break from having to do it myself."

Lauren threw him a mighty blow on his shoulder, nothing like the friendly punches she usually gave Annie. Still, Keith didn't even seem to notice as he swaggered towards the door. Watching the siblings play fight, Annie wished she had a brother or sister.

But at least she had Lexie. The bout wasn't starting for a while but Lexie was already there, holding one of her homemade signs: "'Tis the season of Anne R. Key!" Wow, it was great having Lexie around again!

Now there was just one person missing.

Just got to the rink. Hope you can still make it. It'd mean a lot to me to have you here! Xx

Annie sent the text to Tyler. She hoped it didn't sound like she was nagging. She'd gone to his championship game, after all; it was only fair that he came to hers.

The scene in the locker room was like a twisted version of Santa's workshop. Holly was Sexy Santa complete with thigh-high stockings, a micro-mini, and a faux fur vest showing a lot of cleavage. Liz was wearing all green and had added pointy elf-ears to her triple-pierced ears. Sharmila was her usual gorgeous self in angel wings and a halo attached to her helmet.

That was the great thing about roller derby: everyone could express themselves however they wanted. As long as there was a visible number on your back and arm, and it was obvious what team you were on, you could wear what you liked. It was brilliant.

Once Sharmila had drawn stars around Annie's eyes to go with the tinsel and the silver leggings she'd bought with Lexie, Annie headed to Jesse's booth to get her skates.

Except they weren't on the counter waiting for her as usual. The last time Jesse didn't have her skates ready was when he thought Annie had given up roller derby for cheerleading. As if. Today, though, he had a smile that said he knew something she didn't.

"What's up?" she asked.

"Nothing." He grinned even wider. "It's just that some elf came by and dropped this off yesterday." From under the counter

Jesse pulled out a box wrapped in metallic paper with a huge red bow on it.

"What?" Annie started to ask, but then got her answer from the familiar handwriting on the package:

To Annie, we're so proud of you! Love from Mum and Dad

"Aww!" She tore off the paper and turned the box on its side to read what it was. "No way, no way!"

She opened the box and pulled out a brand-new black roller skate. Shifting the tissue paper aside, she got out the other skate as well. She held them in her hands, testing their wheels and turning the skates to admire them from every angle.

"Wow, they're amazing!"

"Your dad called me the other day to ask for a recommendation." Jesse couldn't keep the pride out of his voice. "Apparently your mom was determined to get you a new pair for Christmas. I told him these here were a bit pricey, but would last forever."

"They're perfect!" Annie flung her arms around him and dashed off to try them on. They were a little stiff around the ankle, particularly on her left side with the brace. Thank goodness she had thick socks on to avoid blisters. Still, the footbed was cushioned and already they felt better than the rental skates. There wasn't really any difference using them on the carpet, but she couldn't wait to test them on the wooden floor.

But that would have to wait.

"Gather round girls," Coach Ritter called them over. They put their arms around each other and stood in a tight huddle. "I just want to say how thankful I am to have all of you on my team. You are all truly spectacular young ladies who have really given it your all. As far as I'm concerned, we've already won. We came together as a team, and that's what counts. Whatever happens, we always have each other. Now, let's show those High Rollers how it's done!"

Arms squeezed across shoulders as the team gave themselves a group hug and cheered. This was it. They were ready!

Annie noticed the smoothness of her new skates as she glided onto the rink. No matter how well Jesse maintained the rental skates, they weren't nearly as good as these new ones. Her parents rocked!

"Nice wheels!" Lauren skated up next to Annie. As if it were planned, they both suddenly changed directions and kept up talking going backwards. "Are they the S500 models? They're killer. Great wheels for speed, sturdy trucks, and comfortable boot. According to the Real Wheels blog, they're the top pick of skaters and refs." Lauren talked up the skates like some people would a car.

Annie grinned. "I'll take your word for it. All I know is that I love them more than anything else right now."

"Don't let lover boy hear you say that."

Annie's head immediately jerked up to the stands. She first found Dad next to Lexie, Lexie's arty friends Aaron and Becky, and two cute kids with flaming red hair − Abbey and Brandon,

Coach Ritter's children. They all waved like crazy fans as soon as she glanced at them. She waved back and kept searching for Tyler. She almost overlooked him. He was in the top row of the stands, tucked away in a corner with his head down, undoubtedly playing games on his phone. She started to call out to him, but then changed her mind. It was only the warm-up. Let him play his game until the bout started.

Liz and Holly led the team in some warm-ups using dance moves to Jesse's Christmas rock soundtrack. During the Smashing Pumpkins' slow "Christmas Time", the team glided through grapevines crossing a skate in front and then behind the other in a sideways step. Then it was free dance to the Ramones' "Merry Christmas (I Don't Want to Fight Tonight)". No synchronization, just letting it loose and having fun. Just how it should be.

"Ladies and gentlemen, folks of all ages," Jesse bellowed into the mike, "have we got the bout of the year for you this evening. Tonight, we have the reigning champions here to see if they can keep hold of their title for a fourth year against a team that came out of nowhere. Please give it up for the High Rollers and the Liberty Belles!"

The crowd cheered like crazy and kept it up as the individual players were introduced, the High Rollers first.

"She's a demon on wheels, number six six six, Deeeeeeeeee Stroyer!"

Annie watched as her biggest rival whipped around the track at high speed. When she got back to the rest of her team, Dee Stroyer sliced a finger across her neck at the Liberty Belles.

Instantly, Liz pulled down Holly's hand which had shot up to give Dee the finger. Annie locked eyes with her nemesis and shook her head.

You're not going to psych us out this time. We're better than that. Just you watch.

"Remember, girls, we fight with points, not fists," Coach Ritter said. "And no language! My children are out there."

Coach looked pointedly at Holly who had in past bouts been sent to the box for bad-mouthing an opposing player and insulting a ref.

"Don't worry, I'm good." Holly waved the concern away. "They won't get what I'm saying tonight. Thanks to my teammates, I can swear in Spanish and Hindi!"

When Jesse introduced Annie, he switched the music to Madonna's "Lucky Star". She skated around the track at her usual top speed. With the song blaring, Annie knew what she had to do. She took a deep breath and sent her body into an aerial – a hands-free cartwheel. The crowd roared as she landed smoothly back on her skates.

Annie joined the rest of her team who were standing with their arms around each other as Holly did her signature double axel. Annie looked at the High Rollers whose benches were on the other side of the penalty box, and smiled sweetly at her nemesis. *See, Dee? Now that's real intimidation. Teamwork.*

They settled down on the benches once all the introductions were finished. Coach held the jammer's starred helmet panty as she looked at the team. Usually she started the bout with Liz or

163

Holly as jammer. This time she threw the panty at Annie, who caught it in one hand.

Brilliant!

Except that right next to her on the jammer line was Dee Stroyer.

"Ready to get clobbered?" Dee muttered under her breath as they both crouched down low.

"Not a chance," Annie said a second before the two short whistles indicated the jammers' start. Annie took off towards the pack, Dee Stroyer at her heels.

The Belles' blockers were Liz, Lauren, Sharmila, and Bea. Like a magic curtain, they cleared the smallest gap in the wall. Annie sucked in her breath and skated through sideways. A quick glance under her arm showed the gap had disappeared and Lauren had just knocked Dee to the ground.

Fast, fast, fast, legs crossing over, Annie caught up with the pack again. Dee had got back to her feet, made it through the pack, and was halfway around the track. In a few seconds she could start scoring points if she passed any of the Belles.

Not happening.

Annie barged her way between two burly blockers and as soon as she cleared the pack again, she tapped her hips to call off the jam. Back at the bench, she saw the score change to 4-0. Not much of a lead, but Annie took it as a sign of many more points to come.

And she was right.

In the next jam, Holly scored six points, and Annie somehow

refrained from telling the High Rollers to read it and weep as the score changed to 10-1. In the jam after that, the score remained the same.

Annie was sent out as a blocker twice before she played jammer again. The next time she crouched at the jammer line the player next to her was a black-haired girl called Cruella de Kill.

Amongst the blockers in front of her, Annie spotted Dee Stroyer wearing the pivot panty. Not only would Dee set the pace of the pack, she would also tell the other girls on her team what to do. Annie tried not to think about that. When the jammers' whistle blew, Annie headed straight for the middle of the blockers. At the last second she veered to the left to try and sneak by on the inside but she got pushed out of bounds. She came back behind the pack and searched for another gap. There weren't any. Her teammates were busy blocking Cruella and couldn't help her. Right, she'd have to barge her way through.

She pressed against the pack but someone knocked into her and Annie's new skates whipped out from under her. She landed hard on her thigh, but got right back up again.

The next thing Annie knew, Dee Stroyer and Cruella de Kill were both skating on the out-of-bounds track towards the penalty box. With Cruella out for a minute, there was no opposing jammer to score points, and with one blocker down, Annie could break through the pack much more easily. It was a power jam – a brilliant opportunity to score loads of points!

Lauren, as the Belles' pivot, kept the pack from moving as

much as possible, while Carmen, Tashi, and Cookie helped Lauren block the opposing team's remaining blockers. Annie lapped the Rollers once, twice, and three times! Speeding around the track, Annie knew that any second, Dee and Cruella would be released from the sin bin, and she wanted to pass the pack one more time before that happened.

Lauren held out her arm just as Annie was approaching the pack for the fourth time. Annie grabbed it and with a mighty heave, Lauren whipped her around. The momentum caused Annie to catch some air and the curve of the track added a twist. Without planning it, she brought her legs out to the sides in a straddle, touched the toes of her new skates, and twisted a full turn before landing smoothly.

The crowd roared their approval.

Just in front of her, Dee and Cruella were rushing out of the box. Annie decided to play a cat and mouse game as they raced to catch up with the pack. Just before the two returning High Rollers had caught up with the pack, Annie called off the jam. It was annoying for them but totally legal. In that jam alone, Annie had scored twenty points while the High Rollers had scored none. Brilliant!

"A great power jam by Anne R. Key, bringing the score to fifty-seven to twenty-four," Jesse announced.

Dad, Lexie, and Coach Ritter's kids all cheered. Annie waved and turned to blow a kiss to Tyler. Except he was still staring at his phone. Annie pressed her lips together. What was the point in coming to the bout if he wasn't going to watch her play?

Whatever. The bout was too exciting to worry about that now.

The Belles kept their lead and by halftime were almost fifty points ahead. Dee Stroyer was livid but couldn't do anything about it; the Liberty Belles were creaming the High Rollers, fair and square.

Coach Ritter clapped her hands. "What a way to show them, peeps. All your hard work is paying off. You really look like a team."

In the second half, the gap between the teams narrowed a bit. There was one moment when Annie was a blocker and she was sure the Belles were going to lose their lead. Holly couldn't slow down fast enough, and accidentally back-blocked one of the other blockers, which was illegal.

"Oh no! The Liberty Belles' jammer, Holly Terror, gets sent to the box, which sets Dee Stroyer up for a power jam!" Jesse spoke quickly.

Annie could hear the panic in Jesse's voice as she looked over her shoulder for Dee. She knew that Dee would be out for revenge, but at least Annie was ready for her.

"Dee Stroyer is coming around but the Belles are not giving in easily. Anne R. Key shifts around Lauren Disorder and gives Dee Stroyer a mighty booty block. The High Rollers are trying to help their jammer through, but so far the Belles are looking rock solid."

Liz blocked the Rollers' pivot while Sharmila sent another blocker to her knees. Dee seemed determined to barge her way past Annie, but Annie and Lauren were working together perfectly – just like they had in the Gruesome Twosome drill.

"And there goes the whistle," Jesse said. "In this not-so-powerful jam the High Rollers increased their score by six points."

The audience didn't need an announcer to tell them that this was a disappointing result. In a rage, Dee screamed swear words and threw her helmet towards the bench, narrowly missing an NSO. The five refs all blew their whistles and tapped both hands to their shoulders to call an official timeout. They conferred for a few seconds before the head ref tapped her opposite shoulder, swept the hand across her chest, and jerked her right thumb over her shoulder.

"Ooh, and it looks like Dee Stroyer has been ejected from the bout for gross misconduct. She won't be allowed to sit with her team for the rest of the evening," Jesse said.

Holly, back from the penalty box, looked like Christmas had come early. "I will not rub it in her face, I will not rub it in her face! But dang it feels good!"

Now there was no doubt in Annie's mind that they were going to win. Dee Stroyer was the Rollers' best jammer and with her out of action, and the Belles' substantial lead, victory felt almost certain. But Annie reminded herself not to get overconfident. It was still possible for the Rollers to win.

5:27 minutes left and Annie couldn't stand still. The Belles were thirty-three points ahead. There was still a slight chance they might lose if the High Rollers got another power jam, or if a few Belles got sent to the box. But instead the Belles widened their lead to forty points.

3:41 and Carmen was doing a happy dance by the bench.

With one jam left, there was still the smallest chance the High Rollers could catch up. It was possible. But they didn't. The whistle blew, signalling the end of the bout, and the season.

"And that's it folks. Final score is one hundred and forty-five to ninety-seven. The Liberty Belles, who last year came bottom of the league, are your new league champions! Congratulations to all our roller girls!" Jesse switched from the Christmas songs to Queen's "We Are the Champions" as the Liberty Belles skated their victory lap with huge grins on their faces. When Liz was handed the trophy, there were tears in her eyes.

They had won, they had *won*! Annie still couldn't believe it. It was like a dream come true.

"Everybody get together. I need to take a photo." Sharmila's dad waved them into the middle of the rink. They all stood with their arms around each other, except for Holly who had to pose in front with the trophy.

All the other parents, including Dad, snapped pictures too.

"Can you email that photo to Mum, please?" Annie said to Dad, as he pulled her into a huge hug. She wanted Mum to know the good news straight away.

"You got it, champ," Dad said.

Annie got hugs from Lexie and her friends, Coach's kids, Jesse and his little sister Katie, and even Keith, before she got a chance to dash to the person she most wanted to celebrate with.

As she approached, Tyler slid his phone back into his pocket. It was an awkward hug and when Annie leaned over to kiss him,

169

he turned his head so she got his cheek instead.

"Did you see me score?" Annie teased as she repeated what Tyler often asked her after his matches. Her Cheshire cat smile wasn't going to disappear anytime soon. "Twenty points in that power jam. And a straddle spin."

He didn't even try to look excited about her role in the victory. "Yeah, you were great. Get out of those weird clothes and let's go. The guys are waiting for us."

A few weeks ago, Annie would have rushed to do his bidding. But now she could only hear him being bossy.

The glory of being a league champion dwindled as anger rose up in Annie's chest. She knew he had been texting or playing on his phone for most of the bout, but she'd given him the benefit of the doubt and hoped he'd looked up a few times. She folded her arms across her chest and shook her head. "No, I'm heading to Rosie Lee's. It's our Christmas party, and now our championship celebration too. I told you about it ages ago."

Tyler shook his head. "No you didn't."

Annie took a deep breath, trying to calm herself down. She could find the text and show him, but she didn't want to be that kind of girlfriend. Better take the conversation a different route. "Why don't you join us?"

"I'm not hanging out with a bunch of freaks!" Tyler said loudly enough for several people to turn and stare at him, including Holly and Sharmila, who looked ready to use their toughest blocking moves on Tyler.

Annie crossed her arms over her chest. "These 'freaks' are

some of my best friends."

Tyler let his arms flop to his side in exasperation. "Look, I let you play roller derby tonight, but now it's time to hang out with my friends."

Let me play? No, sorry, mate. "You can go if you like, but I'm staying."

Tyler's green eyes flashed in anger. For the first time since Annie had known him, she didn't find him attractive. He leaned over and hissed, "If you choose to hang out with them over me, we're over."

What? Really? Annie didn't even hesitate with her answer. "Fine. Be that way."

It took a second for Tyler to understand what she was saying. His cheeks flushed. "No one turns me down. You're going to regret it."

"No, I'm not." Annie lifted her chin up with more certainty than defiance. "Anyone who puts down my friends insults me too."

Tyler's face got even uglier and Annie couldn't think of a single reason why she ever liked him. "You're just as big a freak as the rest of them."

"Cheers," Annie said without sarcasm. She watched Tyler, her ex-boyfriend now, storm out of the rink. Immediately, Lexie and Lauren appeared out of nowhere and put their arms around her. She'd loved being his girlfriend, but Tyler Erickson had never been a true friend.

Chapter Eighteen

"How're you holding up?" Lexie asked as she artistically arranged cookies on a plate. Dad had driven the two of them back to Rosie Lee's to get things ready for the Christmas party; the rest of the team would be there in about ten minutes.

Annie turned off the steam wand and poured the hot milk into a large carafe. "I'm a bit sad, but I'll be fine. I'm more bothered by how stupid I was around him. I think I liked being his girlfriend more than I liked him. Does that make any sense?"

"No, but I'm glad you're handling it well. It'd be horrible if you got all mopey and stopped eating and all."

Annie laughed and filled the jug with more milk to steam. "My dad is the best cook in the world. It'd take more than a bad break-up to get me to stop eating."

"Excuse me?" Dad called out from the kitchen. "Best cook in the world? Try the entire universe, and then you might be closer to the truth."

Annie turned the knob of the steamer so she wouldn't have to burst Dad's bubble. She wasn't lying about Tyler though. OK, so she loved how gorgeous he was, and it had been really flattering that he'd asked her out. They'd had some fun times together. When he wasn't putting down her friends. Or always demanding that they do what he wanted them to do. Or trying to prove he was fitter than she was. Now that she really thought about it, he wasn't very nice. Next time she got a boyfriend, he wasn't just going to be hot – he'd better be nice, too.

Annie poured the last of the steamed milk into the carafe and got a long-handled wooden spoon to make sure all the chocolate had dissolved into the milk before sealing it tight. The carafe held around twenty-four mugs of hot chocolate – just about enough for a team of hungry roller girls.

Dad came out of the kitchen with a huge bowl of whipped cream. "I took your advice and made peppermint whipped cream for the hot chocolate. Absolutely no touching it until everyone's here."

As soon as Dad went back to the kitchen, Annie handed Lexie a spoon and grabbed one for herself. Checking to make sure Dad couldn't see them, they both sneaked a taste. It was pure heaven. The peppermint wasn't too overpowering and the cream had a subtle vanilla undertone. Forget the hot chocolate, Annie could have eaten the whole bowl of whipped cream on its own.

She was saved from temptation by the door jingling open; Lauren and Jesse were the first arrivals. Then came Coach Ritter with her two kids. The rest of the team arrived within minutes. Liz walked in with the trophy. She set it on display at a central table and every once in a while checked to make sure it was still there.

"I overheard you and the soccer god." Holly made a rude gesture before grabbing a handful of white-chocolate-covered pretzels. "What a jackass. Just saying, anybody who disses you, and your friends, is not cool. Screw his good looks."

"Thanks." Annie knew by the way gossip flew, there wasn't anyone in Liberty Heights who didn't know that the soccer captain and the English girl were no more. Might as well get used to being single.

Everyone got served hot chocolate (Lexie helped Annie shape the peppermint whipped cream into beautiful mounds) and the cookies made several rounds.

"Oh my god, this is sooo good," Lauren moaned as she tried the hot chocolate.

Liz agreed. "And these are the best cookies ever."

Annie waited for Dad to buff his fingers against his shirt or brag that he had taught Martha Stewart everything she knew, but nothing. He wasn't even in the café area. Weird. She hoped he wasn't prepping for tomorrow. The party was supposed to be chill time for everyone. One workaholic parent was more than enough.

The door to the café jingled open and Annie was just about

to tell the customer that they were closed, when a white-bearded man in a red and white suit poked his head in.

"Ho, ho, ho! I hear we have some roller derby champions in the house. Is that so?" Santa asked.

"Yeah!" the girls all cheered.

"Well, then. I think I might have some presents for you." Santa let himself in and heaved a flour bag off his shoulder. Annie grinned. Where could "Santa" have possibly found such a convenient sack for his loot?

Abbey and Brandon dashed up to him. "Do you have anything for us?"

Santa leaned over his huge belly to look at Coach Ritter's kids. "My, my. You must be part of the junior team. Let's see what I've got for you."

He pulled out two presents: remote control cars, one green and one red. The kids loved them and were immediately driving them around the café. Lauren and Carmen even looked a tiny bit jealous.

"And for the rest of you, I got a special shipment from my elves." Santa started handing out the presents from the team's Secret Santa exchange.

Sharmila squealed when she opened the make-up kit Annie had bought for her and immediately started trying it out.

Lauren wouldn't let go of the basset hound stuffed animal Liz gave her.

Holly freaked out at the hot pants on which Carmen had ironed-on the word "Kickass" in big letters across the bum.

Even though Lexie wasn't a roller girl, Annie had got her best friend a new set of colouring pencils just like ones she'd been using when Annie and Mum had gone running in the park.

Coach Ritter got a box of chocolate truffles that Annie suspected were homemade by "Santa" himself.

Annie opened her present slowly, savouring the moment. She knew what it was from the shape, but didn't know exactly what it held.

"Total Anne R. Key", the CD label said, listing songs she had never heard even though they were by some of her favourite bands. She put the CD on right away. OK, so the gifts were meant to be from a "secret" Santa, but only one person could have put something like that together.

Jesse was wearing his present, a black bandana with skulls, and was nodding to the music when Annie came up to him.

"Nice tunes," he said.

"Yeah," Annie said. "Somebody in this room must have really good taste."

"Introduce me when you find out who it is." Jesse grinned mischievously like he had when he gave Annie her new skates.

Annie gave him a quick hug and whispered in his ear, "Thanks! You rock!"

Santa's booming voice carried across the café. "Oops, looks like someone's under the mistletoe."

Annie quickly broke away from Jesse. But it wasn't her, rather Coach Ritter, who was staring at the branch above her head. Santa stuck out his cheek and tapped it with a finger. Instead,

Coach Ritter grabbed him by the furry collar and pulled him in for a real kiss. With the whole team cheering, Santa wrapped his arms around her and kissed her back.

Annie collapsed into a chair. *It's just mistletoe. It doesn't mean anything.* But who was she kidding? She wasn't young like Coach's kids (who were still playing with their cars and hadn't noticed a thing). Annie had seen it coming. But even though she was OK with it, it still made her feel strange. Coach Ritter wasn't Mum.

She felt a squeeze on her shoulder and reached up to hold Lexie's hand. What would she do without her best friend?

"Boy, it's hot in here." Santa pulled at the collar of his red suit to let some air in. The team kept cheering and making cheeky comments about why the temperature had risen. Santa smiled sheepishly, grabbed the empty flour bag, and disappeared into the back. A few minutes later, Dad reappeared as if nothing had happened. "Sorry, guys, I must have dozed off. Did I miss anything?"

Coach Ritter winked. "I'll fill you in later. But for now I've got a few gifts of my own for the team."

She pulled out a folder from her bag. "I don't have them in any order, it's just how they were printed out. Holly gets the 'Life of the Party Award', for always keeping us from taking the sport too seriously."

Holly held the certificate against her chest and wiped pretend tears from her eyes. "I'd like to thank my momma and poppa for believing in me, and all those little people I had to roll over to get to where I am today."

ments, and insults, flew good-naturedly as Holly
back to her seat.

he 'Most Feared Award' goes to Lauren."

Everyone laughed as Lauren accepted her award with the
stuffed dog still in her hand. On the rink she might have been the
hardest blocker to get by, but off the rink she was a softie.

"For Liz, our captain, I have the 'Most Valuable Player Award',
for leading the Liberty Belles to their first ever championship
victory."

The whole café erupted into cheers and whistles that took
several minutes to quieten down. Once everyone had settled
again, Coach continued handing out awards to everyone else on
the team. Except Annie.

*Maybe she forgot to print mine. Maybe it slipped out of the folder
and she didn't notice.*

"And last, but not least, I talked with the other coaches and
we all agreed that the league-wide award for 'Rookie of the Year'
goes to Annie."

"Yeah it does!" Jesse screamed while Lauren stuck two fingers
in her mouth for an ear-piercing whistle.

"I still remember when you crashed into the barrier because
you didn't know how to stop," Liz said as she gave Annie a hug.
Annie remembered it well. It had been the first day of the Fresh
Meat workshop that had taught her how to play roller derby. *I
can't believe I was that bad just a few months ago.*

She took her certificate and gave her widest smile while
Dad took a picture. Somehow she got the feeling that either

the picture or the certificate, or both, would end up on the wall at Rosie Lee's.

The party settled down after that with the girls going over the highlights of the season and helping themselves to more goodies. When Brandon fell asleep with his hand still clutching his car remote control, everyone started packing up and arranging lifts home. Dad carried Brandon to Coach's car and didn't return for a good while. Annie didn't ask but got the feeling that "Santa" hadn't been the only person Coach Ritter kissed tonight.

After the team left, Annie, Lexie, and Dad worked quickly to get the place all tidied up.

"Dad, I forgot to thank you for the skates earlier," Annie said as she swept the last crumbs. "They're amazing. I know they weren't cheap."

Dad held the dustpan in place for Annie to sweep into it. "They're from your mother too. We're both very proud of you. You've grown so much."

Annie playfully shoved him. "No, don't say that! I don't want to change my derby number. Six foot isn't nearly as cool as five foot eleven and a half."

"You know what I meant, Beanie," Dad scolded playfully. It wasn't often Annie beat him to a tease. "I wouldn't have thought it, but I'm really glad you joined the roller derby league instead of cheerleading or basketball. It's been a great sport for you."

"And let's not forget who introduced you to that great sport," Lexie said as she came out of the kitchen with the mop bucket.

Annie held out her arm in presentation. "The one and only

Alexis Raquel Jones."

Lexie bowed deeply and repetitively. "Thank you, thank you. Just so you know, as your agent, I have the right to twenty per cent of all your future earnings."

"Hey, if she gets twenty per cent, then I should at least get fifty per cent for raising you," Dad said as he emptied the crumbs in the bin.

Annie pretended to grumble then grinned. "How about VIP passes to my first professional bout?"

"Deal!" Dad and Lexie said at the same time and they all laughed. Dad went back into the kitchen while Annie insisted on taking over the mopping. Without needing to be asked, Lexie shifted the tables out of the way and returned them to their usual spots after Annie had mopped each area.

When the girls had finished, Lexie seemed to start gathering up her things.

"Aren't you sleeping over?" Annie asked, wondering if she had said or done something wrong.

"Of course I am. I just wanted to give you your Christmas present." Lexie hid something behind her back for a few seconds before revealing it to Annie.

"You—" Annie started to say that Lexie didn't have to give her anything, but then she saw what it was and all words left her.

It was an oil painting of two women on a park bench, one with wild ringlets and the other with long legs stretched out in front of her. Annie recognized them instantly – the smiling faces were her and Lexie, except there was an older look about both of them.

"Is this us all grown-up?" Annie asked.

Lexie shrugged and looked a bit sheepish. "Kind of. I was imagining us hanging out together when we're older in some exciting place like New York or London. I know that's kind of silly, but—"

Annie didn't let her friend finish. She set the painting down and flung her arms around Lexie. Even after how Annie had treated her over the last few weeks, Lexie wanted them to stay friends for years? It was like winning the championship bout all over again. "I love it!"

"Really?" Lexie sounded like she couldn't believe her ears.

Annie nodded. After all that had happened recently, Annie knew that you really couldn't predict the future. A year ago she wouldn't have believed that her parents would be divorcing, she'd be living in America and crazy about a sport played on roller skates. But she did know one thing for certain: she was going to do everything she could to make sure Lexie stayed in her life for a very long time. "Absolutely. You're the best friend in the whole world and we've got years of fun ahead of us."

"Here's to the future us!" Lexie said, raising an empty mug in a mock toast.

"To the future us!" Annie cried out happily. The future was fun to think about, but the present was pretty great too. "And to us right here, right now."

"You're right," said Lexie with a big grin. "We do make a pretty awesome team."

ALL ABOUT Roller Derby

RULES OF THE GAME

A roller derby game is called a bout. A bout usually lasts sixty minutes and is divided into two-minute jams. During a jam, each of the two teams have five players on the track, all skating in the same direction. The blockers and pivots form a tight pack. The two jammers start behind them and race to break through the pack. The first jammer through the pack is designated the lead jammer. However, no points can be scored until the jammer passes the pack for a second time. The jammer then scores a point for every opponent that she overtakes, provided she passes the player in bounds and without penalties. Both jammers may score points for the duration of the two-minute jam or until the lead jammer calls off the jam. A jammer typically scores four points every time she makes it through the pack. If she overtakes the other jammer she scores a fifth point, and this is known as a Grand Slam. The team with the most points at the end of the bout wins.

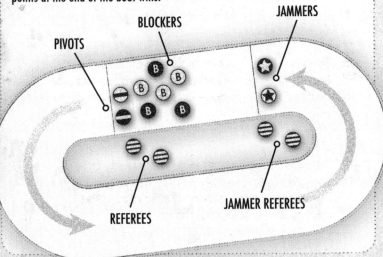

JAMMERS

BLOCKERS

PIVOTS

JAMMER REFEREES

REFEREES

SKATER POSITIONS

  JAMMER

The jammer wears a helmet cover with a star and is the only player who can score points. To score points, a jammer must break through the pack once and sprint around the track. A jammer scores a point for every opponent she passes on her subsequent passes through the pack.

LEAD JAMMER

The lead jammer is the first jammer to break through the pack and pass all the opposing blockers and pivot. The lead jammer may choose, at a strategic time, to call off the jam to prevent the opposing jammer from scoring. She does this by putting her hands on her hips.

  PIVOT

The pivot acts as a pacesetter for the team and is designated by a striped helmet. The pivot calls out plays and provides guidance for the rest of the team. The pivot typically stays in front of the blockers.

  BLOCKER

Each team has three blockers on the track. The blockers play both offensive and defensive roles. They help their jammer get through the pack, while trying to prevent the opposing jammer from getting through.

PENALTIES

There are many rules in the sport of roller derby, enforced by referees and non-skating officials (NSOs). If a skater commits a major penalty, she is sent to the penalty box, also known as the sin bin, for sixty seconds. If a jammer is sent to the penalty box, the opposing team's jammer scores a point for the missing player if she passes through the pack. If both jammers are sent to the penalty box, the first jammer is released as soon as the second jammer reaches the box.

OFFENCES RESULTING IN A MAJOR PENALTY INCLUDE:

- ☒ Tripping an opposing player
- ☒ Back blocking
- ☒ Using elbows to the chest or face
- ☒ Swearing at another skater or referee
- ☒ Blocking twenty feet ahead or behind the pack
- ☒ Deliberately falling in front of another player
- ☒ Grabbing, pulling or pushing an opposing player

HISTORY OF ROLLER DERBY

Roller derby was first played in the 1930s and quickly evolved into a popular spectator sport, thanks to staged crashes and collisions. By 1940 it was watched by about five million spectators, but by the 1970s the sport had faded into obscurity. At the beginning of the twenty-first century, a roller derby revival began in Austin, Texas and soon spread to many other cities and countries. Modern roller derby has focused on athleticism rather than showmanship. It is the fastest-growing sport in America, and is under consideration to become an Olympic sport at the 2020 games!

Hooked on roller derby?

Here are three more fast and furious *Roller Girls*
books about Annie and her friends.

Falling Hard

After Annie Turner's parents split up, she thought moving to the USA with her dad would be an exciting new start. But she's struggling to fit in. For a start, the most popular girl at school hates her! Things finally begin to look up when Annie discovers the wild sport of roller derby and a whole underground scene she'd never even known existed. And then there's Tyler, a green-eyed football player who literally makes Annie want to drool in public...

Is Annie tough enough to make it as a roller girl?

Hell's Belles

Annie Turner's roller derby team, the Liberty Belles, is finally
on a winning streak. Full of confidence, the girls plan a
Halloween bout with the High Rollers, their tough and cheeky
arch-rivals. There'll be costumes, gruesome make-up and plenty
of trash talk to look forward to. But when Annie's crush asks
her to a Halloween dance on the same night, she finds herself
torn between her girls and her man.

Will Annie's first American Halloween turn
out to be more 'trick' than 'treat'?

Boot Camp Blues

Annie Turner is single again and it really kind of sucks. It doesn't help that her ex is now going out with a cheerleader! But she's also confused by her new feelings for skater boy Jesse. They're just friends … aren't they? Meanwhile, Annie and her roller girls are each desperate to make the cut for an all-star team. Tensions run high as the teammates compete against each other for roller glory.

**Will the stars in Annie's eyes get
in the way of her friendships?**

For more exciting books from brilliant
authors, follow the fox!
www.curious-fox.com